Becca's Ghost

Lorrain Everett

DEDICATION

This book is dedicated to Mini Me and Little Man, though you are way to young to read my books you have always put up with my moods when the characters weren't doing what I wanted, and you were never ashamed to tell people that I write 'mommy porn' . To my best friend/sister Tulip May, thanks for being honest when I was being dull, and for having faith that I could turn a short story into something more. To H.D. for helping make the 'spy stuff' a little more realistic, and for being my inspiration for the fun stuff too. Last but not least, to my Mom & Dad, I pray you never read this book but thanks for keeping on your bookshelf!

"YOU KNOW YOU'RE IN LOVE WHEN YOU CAN'T FALL
ASLEEP BECAUSE REALITY IS FINALLY BETTER THAN
YOUR DREAMS."
— DR. SEUSS

ACKNOWLEDGMENTS

Thankful for the characters who live in my imagination and sometimes let me put their lives onto paper.

1 CHAPTER NAME

The bar had the normal people sitting around the normal table having the normal conversation. The only difference was that I noticed HIM. He had never been there before. I was normally sitting on the opposite end of the table watching the people, almost my favorite pastime. Tonight, my seat was taken by some guy who smelled really bad so I moved up the table closer to the middle. He was talking politics and religion with everyone else, normally I didn't pay attention to the conversation to much but his voice was deep and sexy. I really didn't have a choice but to listen!! Making the decision to be brave I started thinking of ways to introduce myself to him. I went up to the bar for some liquid courage, when I headed back to the table he was gone!! Thinking I had lost my chance I finished my drink and headed home.

For the next week, all I could think about was how

sexy he was. Pretty sure my friend Christy got tired of hearing it. Now don't get me wrong. I was still going to class and work but all my free time was spent fantasizing about him. That Friday I was lazing on my bed studying when Christy opened the door – "Why aren't you getting dressed?"

"Dressed for what?"

Christy rolled her eyes at me, "I bought two dresses today so we can go get your dream guy." She held up two very short, very sexy dresses, one red and one black.

I sat up and took the red one from her. "Do you really think he'll be there tonight? He was never there before. Maybe it was a fluke?"

"If it was a fluke then we'll look amazing and you'll meet someone else, if he is there then…. well, you can figure out that part on your own!"

About an hour later we were headed down town. Reno's wasn't one of those meat markets like you find in most college towns, there were the regulars from town who were always there and then a steady stream of college students who had a beer or two before they realized they weren't going to pick up some easy bimbo for the night and moved on down the street.

I went up to the bar to get us some wings and a pitcher of beer while Christy found us a table near the dart boards. I had just sat down the plate of wings and was licking some sauce off my thumb when he walked in. He had on black jeans that hugged his perfect ass and a black polo shirt that showed off his amazing shoulders. I'm pretty sure everyone froze to watch him walk across the bar, ok maybe it was just me, but wow, really WOW!

"Becky look by the door, he's here. Oh, never mind you saw him." I could hear Christy laughing at me as she put her beer down and headed toward him.

Wait, what? Why was she walking over there? Now she was talking to him and pointing in my direction!! Crap they were coming over!

"Rick this is my friend Becky. Becky this is our new friend Rick. I'll leave you two to get acquainted."

Recovering from my shock I offered my hand. "Hi, I'm Becky Norton, nice to meet you. Sorry about Christy, she can be so blunt sometimes."

"No problem, she's sweet to try to set you up. I'm Rick Dorsey. Nice to meet you too. I was going to talk to you last week but I got a phone call that ran long and you were gone when I came back." So, he had seen me. As we exchanged pleasantries I checked him out. About 6' 4", beautiful tan skin, black hair, deep green eyes and the sexiest smile I had ever seen, he cut a hot figure in those pants too.

Rick checked me out while we were talking too. Shoulder length auburn curls, green eyes and a cute little 20-year-old body, in the red dress that Christy picked out I knew I looked hot that night. I could read it in his eyes when he made the decision to ask me out. His next words shocked me for a moment.

"I'm afraid I can't stay tonight, I have an appointment, but I'd like to get to know you better, would you like to go to dinner with me this week?"

I could feel the blush creeping up my cheeks. "Yes, that would be nice." I wrote my number down for him,

Rick put the paper in his pocket then reached for my hand, I expected a handshake, instead he turned it over and gently placed his lips against my palm. Then he turned and walked out of the bar nodding to a friend who joined him on the way out.

He waited a whole 48 hours to call me. We talked for almost an hour then Rick said he'd pick me up at 5 on Friday. When we hung up I laid back on my bed and stared at the ceiling. Rick was so nice and easy to talk to, not to mention sexy as hell. Ok, don't get to excited, just see how the date goes, maybe he's worth getting to know.

Friday at 3:30 I got out of the shower, Christy was still at work. I stood naked in front of my closet. I finally settled on jeans and a sexy blouse. I was just finishing my lip gloss when Rick knocked on the door. I smiled as I opened the door, he was wearing blue pants and a royal blue polo shirt that made his skin look like caramel, I had a sudden image of pulling his shirt off to touch the muscle I can see on his chest. He recovered before I did and held up a single sunflower.

"This is for you, you look amazing." I could almost feel his eyes as they ran over every inch of me.

Blushing quite a bit I smiled "Thank you, but my eyes are up here." When I took the flower my fingers touched his and my body jumped at the heat. "Come on in, I'll put this in some water. What did you have in mind for tonight?"

"Well, this may sound a little weird, but there is a dojo I'm thinking of joining and today is the only day the guy is available to talk to me. Would you be okay stopping by there before dinner?"

"Sounds great. I'm ready when you are."

The small talk came easy as he drove. Once inside I walked around looking at the pictures and trophies while he talked to the owner. "He wants me to show me where I'm at, do you mind? 15 mins' tops."

"Ok, take your time. Is there somewhere I can watch?"

He pointed me to the viewing area then ran off to change into ghee pants from his trunk. The trainer walked him through some warm up then they started to spar. Another woman sat next to me and watched as well. I forgot all about the magazines and the other woman as I stared at the muscles in his naked chest, I had an almost uncontrollable urge to join him in the shower when he was done.

The woman next to me spoke in an awed whisper,

"your boyfriend is beautiful."

Not really listening I answered her, "yes he is." The sweat running down his naked chest and back drew my attention to his rippling muscles. My mind's eye started painting a picture; both of us naked and dripping sweat. When I came back to reality he had stopped fighting and was watching me with a smile and talking to the trainer.

Rick

He managed to focus on the instructor as they worked out, the conversation flowed as he expected, questions, answers: the usual information session. Noticing the sweat on the other man's brow he glanced at the clock. They had been going at this for 45 minutes. He looked over at Becca to determine if she was upset at the delay or not. She was sitting on the edge of her seat with her lips slightly parted. Her deep breathing was obvious as well. But it was her eyes that caught his attention. Her pupils were dilated, she looked like she wanted to devour him right where he stood. He couldn't look away from her.

He was mesmerized by the look on her face. So, enamored was he by the hunger in her eyes that he had no clue if he had just agreed to accept the man's offer or buy a car. Never mind, all the info he needed would be in the packet he would surely find tucked into his gym bag. Never taking his eyes from hers he walked to the chair she was occupying and knelt in front of her, "I'll take a quick shower, then we'll go eat, you look hungry." Even though her face turned a very becoming shade of red she was quick to reply.

"Well hurry, I'm starving." She let her tongue slip out to lick her bottom lip, it was almost his undoing.

In the dressing room, he managed to jump in and out of the shower in 10 minutes. The packet was in his bag as usual. He opened it for a quick check; target, specifics and dossier. He shoved the packet back into the bag under his gym clothes and headed out to the lobby to attempt a normal date with this beautiful woman.

Becca

The restaurant was a little Mexican place where we sat and talked about school, life, music. Everything under the sun. I told him about my dream of opening an interior design shop of my own, he told me about his dream home complete with wrap around porch and 15 acres. I spent a lot of time looking into his eyes, I couldn't help it, they were the most amazing shade of hazel green. We ended up sitting there for several hours just talking. It felt like old friends come together after a long time apart. As the evening wrapped up he got a call and had to step outside. While he was gone, I called Christy.

"He's absolutely perfect!!" I told her about watching him work out, the muscles, the sweat, all of it!

"He sounds fabulous so far. Is he a good kisser?"

"Don't know yet but I fully intend to find out tonight!"

Before I could say anything else Rick came back

into the room, as he approached the table I could tell he had bad news.

He sat down heavily in the chair. He looked pissed. "My uncle is sick and I have to go take care of some things for him. I won't be able to take you out for a while. I'm sorry."

I was disappointed but it couldn't be helped. "It's ok, I can wait. Is your uncle going to be ok?"

"He'll be fine, he forgets that he's old and was trying to break in a new horse. Instead he ended up with a broken ankle which is pretty bad for a rancher. I shouldn't be there more than two weeks." He reached across the table and took my hand. "I'm not sure I can wait that long to see you again." He looked embarrassed at that admission. I really liked that he would miss me. "It's getting late, I should get you home."

We walked hand in hand back to the car and held hands all the way home. We took our time getting there, apparently, it was totally mutual that the evening was a success. I was expecting at least a good night kiss when we reached my porch, but instead he turned my hand over in his and kissed my palm again, this time his lips lingered and I felt the tip of his tongue brush my palm. It was all I could do to breathe. "Mind if I call you while I'm gone?"

"Not at all, call me every night. I'd love to talk to you."

He smiled and walked back to his car. It was going to be a really long two weeks. As soon as I closed the door behind me he pulled away from the house, I dropped my purse and ran to Christy's room. She was awake and must have heard us pull up. She already had ice cream in bowls and Mello Yello in glasses. I plopped down on her bed and couldn't stop smiling.

"Ok, so I guess it was wonderful judging by the silly grin on your face."

"It was great, he was great, the restaurant was

great!"

She was trying to laugh, talk and eat ice cream at the same time. "So, when will prince charming be taking you out again? He isn't moving in yet is he?"

"Actually, that's the only bad part of the night. Apparently, his uncle is a rancher and broke his ankle, so he must go out there for a couple of weeks. But as soon as he gets back we are going out and we are going to talk on the phone while he's gone."

"Broken ankle? Do you believe that or is he a secret agent spy man leading a double life and he wants to start family number two with you?"

"I'd be okay with being wife number 2 in his double life, did you check out his ass in those pants? Yum baby yum!!"

We rambled the rest of the night making entirely rude comments about the value of a sexy ass on men.

Rick

He drove down the street then pulled over, watching the house in the mirrors for a few minutes he was sure no one else was watching her. He hated lying to her. She was the first woman he'd wanted to tell the truth, hell she was the first person he'd wanted to be honest with in years. He seriously considered being honest with her at first but then his brain showed him all the ways that knowledge could turn her against him, and endanger them both. As usual, he kept his mouth shut. He sent her a quick text, "I had a great time, can't wait to see you again. Sweet dreams." Closing the phone, he circled the block once just to be sure then headed home to pack.

His flight left early the next morning. As soon as the plane landed he got a voice mail from Becca, "I had a great time too, was hoping to talk to you before your flight but I guess I missed you. I'm headed into class so I'll talk to you later. Stay safe." On the drive to the hotel he argued with himself about calling her tonight or letting the relationship slide away. He never was any good at real relationships. Knowing it was a losing argument, he was going to call her and continue to see her until she told him to get away.

Once at the hotel he checked into the same hotel he always used when in New York, and under the same name, Thomas Moidja. He went to his room, took a quick shower and changed into the khaki shorts and Hawaiian shirt, basically the uniform of his alter ego. Removing the grate cover from the A/C vent on the wall he pulled out a plain paper bag that he had taped in the wall the last time he was here. Unwrapping the paper bag, he pulled out the plastic wrapped Springfield XDs .45ACP. Not his favorite pistol but by far the best for hiding on his body without notice. Grabbing his baseball cap, sun glasses and book bag he headed for the elevator.

An older woman in a blue business suit walked into

the elevator after him. She looked him from top to bottom. "Nice outfit young man, are you just visiting New York?"

"Yes ma'am, name is Thomas Moidja. Pleased to meet you. Any suggestions of fun sites I should take in?"

She grinned and handed him a tourist book from her brief case. "I work for the tourism commission. There are several great places to see in our fair city." The elevator dinged and the door slid open. "Have a productive visit Thomas."

He took the book and then exited the elevator behind her in the lobby. He headed for the café to look over the book and make a game plan. Settling in a back corner he opened the book and took out the envelope inside. Target photo, bio, and daily schedule, all there, as usual. A typed note also came with this one. "No amount of collateral damage is too much. This target must be processed, regardless of situation, casualties or cost." For a moment, Rick wondered what this poor bastard had done and to whom. He quickly forced that thought from his head. The guy wasn't a person, just a target, most likely a murderer and a general bad guy. Not for the first time in the last few months he questioned this part of his job.

Reading over the schedule he realized his target was out of town until tomorrow night. He ordered lunch and a beer and made out his plan. Usually he just followed the target then took the shot when it presented itself. This time he had a reason to get home as soon as possible. Thinking of her scared the hell out of him. He knew it wasn't safe to want someone as much as he wanted her, she could be used against him. At the same time, her smile made him want to consider other lines of work. He went back to his room, stashed the information and changed for the gym, he needed to release a lot of energy.

Returning from the gym he noticed several obvious security guys wandering the lobby. They seemed to be following a young woman with long black hair and stunning green eyes, she pretended to be oblivious to their presence but he could see the frustration on her face. Smiling to himself he pictured the chaos that would most likely ensue later tonight when that young lady ditched her security team and they had to call 'daddy' to let him know. He imagined it wouldn't be the first or the last time.

Once back in the room he took a shower then called Becca.

"Hey handsome" she sounded very happy to hear from him.

"Hi. How was your day?"

"It was okay. Just work and school. Yours?"

He paused for a moment as he longed to be honest with her. "It was fine, just normal ranch stuff."

He let her do most of the talking because he didn't want to make up more than he had to. When she asked about his parents he was completely honest. "My mom raised me alone, my dad passed away when I was 14. My uncle helped with money but she still worked two jobs to make sure I had everything I wanted. She's living in North Carolina with her sisters now."

"I'm sorry about your dad. It's obvious your mom thought the world of you growing up. Do you get to visit her often?"

"Not nearly often enough, but I plan to see more of her soon. Tell me about your parents."

"Well, they are the typical 'old married couple' they met in high school, married in college, had me, never fight, they whole nine yards. It's sweet but sometimes it's too much."

The conversation flowed, no awkward pauses, no searching for something to say. He liked the sound of her voice way too much. They talked about everything.

Over the next few days he followed the target during the day to get an idea of when to make his move. At night he talked to Becca on the phone. He had never let his two lives mix until he met her. With every conversation, he wanted more and more to get back to her. This trip cost him a lot, emotionally, and he wanted to bury himself in her body and forget New York existed.

Finally, the guy decided to go for a run, just himself and two body guards, through Central Park. Really, he couldn't have made it any easier. He set up his tripod and the extended barrel designed to look like a camera lens, he spent about 20 minutes 'taking pictures' before the target rounded the corner. He had obviously become friends with his body guards and had let his own guard down, they were laughing as they ran, not paying attention to the area; or the dangers around them. Three shots, three bodies, one satisfied client. No viable witnesses. Time to go back to his own life. His flight didn't leave for a few hours so he took a hot shower, cleaned and re-hid the gun behind the grate, then changed into black pants and a black polo.

Rick spent the flight home thinking of Becca and

letting go of what he had just done. It was getting harder with every assignment. He realized these were the bad guys and the country was better off without them. But he was ready to move on to something else. When he accepted this job at the age of 18 he had no idea how he would feel about it now.

Becca

The first date was fabulous, but the second was amazing. He flew in on Thursday and we went out Friday night. Dinner was great, we went to a small steak house, I sat down first in the booth, instead of sitting across from me he scooted in beside me. I smiled as his thigh made contact with mine. I swear I could feel the heat from his skin through my skirt.

He asked if I minded if he ordered for us. I didn't mind so he ordered without even opening the menu. He reached for my hand and rubbed his thumb along my palm as we talked. I tried to pay attention to the conversation but the heat of his hand in mine, and sizzle of his thigh against mine made it very difficult to follow what he was saying. By the time the food arrived I was breathing heavily and all I wanted to do was kiss him. Well, that wasn't all but it was top on my list!

The steak was prime rib but the sauce was unlike

anything I had tasted before. The veggies were seasoned to perfection and the company was sexy as hell. We talked through dinner and enjoyed the comfort of our thighs touching.

The movie was an action film. Something with fighter pilots and lots of sexy scenes. Fast paced and funny. We shared a bag of popcorn. Every time his hand touched mine my stomach fluttered. Even compared to the hot popcorn his hands were warm. I wondered how they would feel on my body, soft and tender or strong and calloused? That thought led to how would he kiss; gentle with a slow building of fire or powerful with an instant passion. Naturally I started thinking of what kind of lover he would be. I no longer cared about the movie, I wanted nothing more than to be alone with this man.

Rick

Rick stole a glance at Becca, she was pretty; not just in a 'girl' way but as a woman; sexy, intense and easy going at the same time. They both reached for popcorn and his hand brushed hers, so soft and subtle. Her fingers lingered beside his for a moment before she withdrew her hand, first he noticed the smile on her face, then he realized she hadn't picked up any popcorn. He wondered if she was thinking along the same lines he was. He put the bag on the seat beside him and turned back toward her. She was looking at him but looked back at the screen when he caught her eyes.

He reached for her hand was only mildly surprised when her fingers curled around his so readily. Rick brought their entwined hands to his lips and placed a soft kiss on the back of her hand. When she looked at him the hunger in her eyes made his body react immediately.

He leaned in and whispered, "I don't even know

what this movie is about anymore. Want to go someplace we can be alone?"

She only paused for a moment before nodding yes. Placing one more kiss on the back of her hand he stood and headed toward the isle. They stepped out into the warm evening air and joined hands as they walked to the car in nervous silence. Both lost in thoughts of where this night would end. Once they were buckled in he realized he didn't know anywhere to go. "Well, this is your town, where are we heading?"

Thinking for a few minutes she grinned suddenly "Are we too old to go to a park? There is a place that is beautiful at night, you can see all the stars, and the water makes wonderful background music."

He nodded, "Sounds perfect. Tell me where to turn as we go."

"Okay, head back toward my house." Once he turned out of the parking lot and into the traffic flow he reached for her hand. He loved the way her much smaller hand fit perfectly into his large hand. As he drove they chit chatted about nothing special and she kept stealing glances at his profile. "Turn right at the next road, follow it until you see the big covered bridge."

He saw the sign for Port Royal State Park a few seconds before the turn. There were only a couple of cars in the small lot so he parked away from them and shut off the engine.

Rick got out and walked around to her side. He opened her door and took her hand to help her out of the car. Becca leaned against the back door in, what she hoped was her best; sexy but innocent, pose. It was clear she wanted him as much as he wanted her.

Seeing her eyes, he wanted to touch her, to kiss her, but this was only the second date, he didn't want to scare her off. He smiled at her and took her hand to pull her against his side, "let's find someplace private to watch the stars."

Putting his passion aside for the moment, he simply enjoyed the physical contact and they walked across the lot toward the old covered bridge.

Built in the 1700s it wasn't meant for cars and was only wide enough for a horse drawn buggy. The walls were solid from the base planks up to about four feet where they opened into large windows with a wide sill of sorts, the perfect size for sitting. They walked to the middle of the bridge and she stepped on the bottom of the railing to look out of the window. At that angle the sexy curve of her bottom was pure torture, he wanted so much to touch her. He leaned against the rail as well and they looked at the stars. "I always wanted to learn about the stars, be able to recognize the constellations, that sort of thing. I just never took the time."

"Which ones do you want to know?" They spent the next little while talking about the stars, she would point out a grouping and he would tell her the name. It was all he could do answer her questions, all his brain registered was the way it felt to have her standing next to him, her arm innocently touching his. He did his best to hide the way his body was reacting to having her this close.

She turned and sat on top of the rail and smiled at him. He could tell by the wicked grin that she was in a flirty mood. He grinned realizing she had known all along exactly the effect she was having on him. He couldn't quite get passed the sweet and innocent vibe he got from her. She certainly knew how to get and keep his attention, but he almost felt like she wouldn't know what to do with him when she had him in her spell. He wanted nothing more than to make love to her right there on that bridge, but for some reason he wanted their first time to be more romantic and tender than just a quickie on the bridge.

Becca

I looked at him and thought how delicious he looked and was determined to get to the kissing part of the date shortly. "Sitting here I'm almost as tall as you."

He stepped directly in front of me, "Almost, but" he stepped forward until his thighs touched my closed knees, "as I get closer the difference matters less and less." His hands rested on top of my denim clad thighs.

Placing my hands over his I opened my knees just wide enough for his hips to fit between them, taking part of his shirt in hand I pulled him close enough to rest my hands on his broad shoulders. Once he was only a few inches from my center I ran my hands from his shoulders to his hands, "If you get close enough, the difference doesn't matter at all."

He turned his hands to take mine, his hands were rough and strong and felt perfect in mine. His eyes were the perfect shade of green, I know he felt my pulse racing. He leaned forward until I could feel his breath on my skin.

"Can I kiss you?" His voice was husky with passion.

"Yes please." I spoke softly so I wouldn't break the spell.

His lips met mine in a soft whisper, tender and questioning yet sure and strong. My breath grew ragged and my heart beat erratic. I released his hands to allow mine to touch his chest, those muscles were tensed and corded beneath my fingers. Running my fingers up to his shoulders again I traced his neck and entwined my hands in his hair. It was soft and thick, as I gently tangled my fingers in his hair his hands began to move as well.

At first his hands rested on my thighs but as the kiss deepened and our passion grew he let them roam up to my waist and under the edge of my shirt.

Rick

The skin of her back was warm and soft and he felt like he could live on that softness alone. He could hardly breathe and hadn't wanted anyone as much as he wanted this woman, right here, right now.

She let her shoes slide off, she slid her bare foot behind his leg and gently tried to pull him closer. He stopped kissing her lips and lifted his head to see her face. Eyes closed, lips parted, head tilted back and skin flushed, she looked so ready to be made love to, he couldn't let her go. He brought his lips to her neck and felt her lean her head away to give him easier access, she made tiny whimpering sounds as he gently nipped the sensitive skin. Placing his hands on her hips he pulled her hard against his need. Even through her jeans and his pants he knew she could feel his hardness. He was as much in need of her as she was of him. Gliding his hands back up to her waist he let his fingers touch the skin above her jeans, then slowly higher and higher until he brushed the underside of her bra. He allowed his thumbs to brush across her lace covered nipples, the reaction was instant. Her nipples hardened into tight little buds that he wanted to expose to the cool night air then suck into his mouth drive her to the edge of reason. She arched against his touch as if she could read his mind and was in total agreement.

From the other end of the bridge came a subtle cough, effectively breaking the spell around them. Rick put his arm around her and let her hide her face against his chest as the other couple walked past. They grinned at him and tried to hurry past. He could feel her shaking and thought she was crying. "It's ok, they're gone." He leaned back to see her face, prepared for tears. When she looked up at him she was laughing.

Becca

Unwilling to let the closeness dissipate I pulled him towards me again with my foot. He felt like perfection pressed against my body. "Good thing they showed up when they did. I had forgotten where we were."

"Me too. A few more moments and that could have been very awkward." I was pleased to hear his voice was still ragged with passion. "Let's walk." He pulled my hips off the rail, my body slid down his until my feet touched the ground. I was left with no doubt that he wanted more, not that he left room for doubt on that front anyway. My breasts cried out for his touch to the point that the movement of the lace bra as we walked was driving me crazy.

He took my hand in his as he stepped back. We walked hand in hand through the park until the moon was high in the sky. When we reached the car we were the only ones in the lot. "I should probably get you home."

I smiled up at him and leaned against the door he wanted to open. Reaching for his shirt, I pulled him against me. "In a few more minutes."

He willingly let me pull him toward my body. He put his hands on my waist and leaned in to caress my lips with his. The contact sent immediate ribbons of fire snaking through my body. His manhood hardened instantly and I could feel him pressing against my belly through his clothes.

Reluctantly he ended the kiss. Taking a deep breath, he tried to speak evenly. "We need to stop now, or I won't be able to."

I smiled and rested my forehead against his chest. "I know that feeling. Guess we should save something for next time."

I stepped away and allowed him to open the door for me. We held hands all the way home. We were both amazed at the power of the instant attraction.

Once at my house he walked me to the door. "Can we go out again?"

"I think we definitely need to do this again." He kissed me one more time then headed back to his car. He sat there until I had gone inside, then he sped down the street.

From that night on we were inseparable. I went to work and classes, he did too but other than that we were together or talking on the phone all the time.

Our third date was a double date with two of his friends. We went to Nashville, had and amazing dinner at the Cheesecake Factory, he confessed his favorite cheesecake was the Jell-O no bake kind out of a box with cherry topping, but these were a close second. Conversation flowed freely around the table. Jon was fairly quiet but opened up toward the end of the meal. Nita and I hit it off and talked the whole time. (it's a woman thing) We took a ride on a horse drawn carriage, then we watched a play put on by a local theater group. We actually saw some of the play, mostly we sat in the back of the crowd and made out. Jon and Nita just laughed at us and made jokes about us getting a room.

He had to go visit his uncle a few more times, but even then, we talked every night. I think it was the fifth or sixth date when I asked him to make love to me. We were at Jon's house, he and Nita were out for the evening. We had pizza delivered, put in a movie and ignored it while we made out in the living room on the couch.

He got up and asked me to wait right there. He got some blankets and pillows, spread them out to make us a pallet on the floor in front of the fireplace, then he started a small fire. He took my hands and stood me up then started undressing me, he kissed and caressed my skin as he uncovered it inch by inch. Once I was completely naked I sat down on the silky camouflage blanket. It felt so good against my naked skin. He looked at me and let his eyes drift slowly from my eyes to my toes then back up. He quickly stripped his clothes from his muscled body. We were both naked on the blanket facing each other, I was suddenly very nervous. Deciding to go after what I needed I crawled toward him until he leaned forward and his mouth captured mine, continuing to move toward his amazing body I straddled him with my hands on his shoulders. His arms were strong and corded, I could feel the muscles trembling with the effort he was putting into sitting still and letting me explore his body. Moving my hands down his chest and across his chiseled abdomen I let my fingers graze the top of his hardened cock. His sharp intake of breath drew my eyes back up to meet his. They were a dark shade of green that gave no hint of the fire burning just beneath the surface. I placed my hands on his shoulders and pushed against him. He laughed quietly, "Do you want me to lay down?" I grinned and nodded yes. I pushed again and this time he laid back on the blanket and I leaned forward and kissed him slowly, building my own heat and working up the courage to kiss my way down his muscled body.

I stopped at his nipples and gently sucked them in turn. He started to reach for me but I sat up "No touching, right now is my turn." He complied with a show of effort. I left a trail of gentle kisses down his stomach. When I reached his erect manhood I felt the first moments pause "You will never fit inside me."

He laughed deep in his chest, "Don't worry baby, your body was made for mine." I hesitated for only a moment more before I placed my tongue at the base and ran it up to the tip. That was the first time I had ever tasted a man, and he was delicious! At first I was tentative, I wasn't sure what he was used to. But after a few moments his body started to react and he moaned in pleasure. I felt the power my mouth had over his cock. I was amazed at the softness of the skin over the rock-solid mass of his penis.

After a few moans he pulled me up against him and rolled

me beneath his body. I opened for him willingly and he

rubbed the head of his cock against my clit before he

slowly worked his way in. I could feel my body stretching

to accommodate his size. He pushed a little farther and

that's when the pain hit, hot, searing pain that made me cry

out. He stopped moving and looked at my face. "You're a

virgin?" I nodded and started trying to move, not sure if I

wanted him closer or out. He leaned his chest down on

mine but kept his hips still. "Baby, be still, let me make this

better for you. No more pain, I promise." I looked into his

eyes as his lips slowly caressed mine. His kiss was soft and

gentle, he slowly started moving again, gyrating his hips

slowly but never going any further than he already had. The

heat started to grow again. He trailed kisses over my neck

as he went a little deeper. I pushed my breasts against his

chest and he sensed my need for more. Joining our lips

again he thrust completely inside me. I had never felt so

full or so complete. I forgot everything about the world around us. The only thing in my world was his body moving over mine. He taught me the meaning of pleasure, gave me my first orgasm, but only the first of many that night.

I was curled up against him drifting in and out of sleep when his phone rang. I started to get up but his arm tightened around me as he answered with the other hand. He spoke in a language I didn't recognize, Arabic I think. I could tell he wasn't happy with the caller but his fingers were drawing little circles on my arm where he held me against his side, so I really wasn't paying much attention.

He hung up the phone and gave me his undivided attention again. I couldn't even think of my own name, much less worry about why he was speaking Arabic on the phone in the middle of the night.

By Christmas we were talking about forever, I only had one more year for my master's degree, he had finished the beginning of December. That's when he went on the trip that started the end of our relationship.

The night he told me the truth he picked me up for a dinner date at Jon's house. His demeanor was off, but I couldn't put my finger on it exactly. The ride over was completely silent. We walked into the house and I realized it was just us, and the table was set for a romantic dinner.

I stopped just inside the door to the kitchen and watched him cooking dinner. "Okay, what's going on?" He turned and looked at me with the most serious look I've ever seen. I went to him and wrapped my arms around his waist. "Whatever it is, we'll work it out. I love you." His hug was almost uncomfortably tight. I started to get scared.

"Ok, sit down with me. I need to tell you a few things I've not been honest with you about." He took my hand and led me to the couch. I felt my stomach starting to churn. "Here goes. All I ask is that you hear me out before you make up your mind."

"I can do that. But you are scaring me baby."

He took a deep breath and told me the truth. "I'm not really a student at Austin Peay. I've been pretending to be a student to infiltrate a group of students that we believe are part of a subversive group." His grip on my hands tightened as if he thought I was going to let go. "I've been with the CIA since I was 18. When I started, I thought I would be spying on bad guys and have this glamorous life. What I really do is hunt bad guys, then stop them, any way possible. I have to leave soon but this will be my last mission." His head was down, almost as if he was afraid to look at me. Not wanting to let go of his hand I leaned forward and kissed the top of his head. He looked up into my eyes. I could see the fear behind his gaze.

"Why couldn't you tell me this before?"

"I wasn't sure I would ever have to. It had started to look like these kids were not who we thought they were. I didn't want you to know any more than need be, I didn't

43

want you in any danger. When I realized, I was falling in love with you I decided you deserved to know the truth before I asked you to marry me. I couldn't go into forever with you with this secret between us."

It took me a few minutes to gather my thoughts. I loved this man with all my heart and wanted to live my life with him. Did his choice of profession really matter? I had grown up around military men, I understood the need to have men who did what he did. I also remembered hearing Mom cry at night when Dad was 'away.' He said this was the last mission though, so he wouldn't be in that kind of danger anymore. Wait, what did that even mean really? He was leaving, that much I got, but how long would he be gone? Would he be in real danger? I looked at his hands, big and strong, I knew he would never let any harm come to me, and I had to trust that he was as good at his job as he was at everything else. Taking a deep breath, I jumped with both feet. "Alright, tell me about what this means. When do you have to leave?"

"I have to go soon, the faster we move on this new intel the better the chance we are able to make a difference in their plans. There are a few things that need to be taken care of to ensure our way of life isn't endangered."

I nodded. "How long will you be gone?"

"I'm not sure baby. If all goes according to plan, we'll be back in a month or so. But I really can't make any promises, I won't know when we'll be home until we're on a plane back."

I took a moment to process that. At least he wasn't making me promises he wasn't sure he could keep. "When you get back you are done right? We'll be free to start our life together?"

"Yes, we have to follow the main boy from the college. Once we take his father my part will be done and I'll be home. I'll be done with the CIA." He looked up at me with sudden surprise, "did you say 'our life together'?"

I couldn't help but smile at his shock. "Of course. I love you and want nothing more than to have a life with you. But no more lies, ever."

"I promise." He dropped to his knees in front of me and pulled a small red velvet box from between the cushions of the couch. "Rebecca Lorrain Norton, you have shown me that love is real and there is hope in the world. Would you do me the honor of becoming my wife?" He opened the box and presented me with a simple, elegant diamond ring.

In spite of the fear in my head, my heart brought tears to my eyes. "Yes Rick! I will marry you." He pulled me into his arms and hugged me as if he'd never let go. That night we laid in his bed cuddled in each other's arms talking about the silly things young newly engaged couples talk about.

The next day he left.

Rick told me he would be gone for a month, but that

turned into a few months and I spent every single day watching the news waiting for any sign of his welfare. I watched the news every morning, went to class, went to work then came home and watched the news some more. The fear and not knowing if he was dead or alive drove me crazy.

It was another rainy day, I had just stepped through my front door and was heading for the TV when the doorbell rang. I opened the door and was immediately swept up in Rick's arms. I started crying with relief. His lips found mine and all the fear and worry of the past few months melted away. He literally growled "I need you." Without setting me down, he closed the door and carried me down the hall to the bedroom. He literally ripped the clothes from my body. He didn't even wait for me to remove his, he stripped faster than ever. Then pushed my knees apart and kissed his way up my thigh. My heart raced as he drew closer to my center, when his mouth closed on my womanhood I screamed with pleasure. I was still reeling back from the edge of orgasm as he kissed a path of fire up my body. He joined his body with mine in one divine stroke. The waves of pleasure washed over us until I felt like I would explode. His fingers entwined in my hair and his hands cupped my head, suddenly I felt more in touch with him than ever before. I was calm but the pleasure was so intense I couldn't understand what was happening. My world was engulfed in the point where his body was joined with mine. Without moving his hands Rick leaned toward me, his kiss was deep and passionate. The love was there but this was a kiss of ownership, the kiss of a man claiming his woman. His orgasm rocked me and I felt the heat of his seed as it too claimed my body.

Softening his kiss and letting his hands slide down my arms he rolled onto his back taking me with him.

Resting my head on his chest and listening to his heart beat I felt whole again. "I'm so glad you are home."

He looked into my eyes. "Me too baby, me too." It was at that moment that I noticed the bruises and the bandages on his shoulder and his rib cage. I gently traced the dressings with a finger and laid my hand over the bruises as if I could will away any pain he went through. He touched my chin and forced my eyes to his. He could see the tears that I was trying not to shed. "I'm ok, I'm home. With you. We are safe. I'll heal and we'll move one." I nodded and laid my head on his chest. We laid in each other's arms both lost in thought until we drifted off to sleep.

Things returned to normal pretty quick. I didn't notice at first how often he looked over his shoulder or double checked the locks on the doors. I did notice how many phone calls he got that he had to leave the room to take, but I chose not to question him. I also noticed that our love making had changed. It was rare that we had quickies or 'fuck' sessions. He touched me like he was scared I was going to break, or vanish.

He'd been home about a month when I walked into his apartment and found him packing, a set of orders on the bed beside the suitcase. "Where are you going?"

I saw the word Afghanistan before he managed to stuff the papers into the case and close it. "I was just about to call you. I have to go. I have no choice. They have one of my men. They have plans to kill thousands. Americans Becky." He must have seen the look on my face. He paused and took my hands in his. "I have to stop them."

Picking anger over fear I jerked my hands out of his and stumbled back away from him. "YOU have to stop them? Are you the only person working for the CIA now? You told me you were out. You said we were free to start our life. You lied to me."

He at least had the decency to look ashamed about lying. "Yes, I have to stop them, it's my job – kill the bad guys Becca that's what I do. It's what I'm good at, damn it baby it's the only thing I'm good at."

I started crying, not from heartbreak (that would come later) but from anger, fear and betrayal. I told him to choose right then. It was wrong, I knew that but my heart spoke before my brain had a chance to weigh in. He hesitated, oh God, why did he hesitate? "You were good at loving me." I threw the engagement ring at him and stormed out. I never turned around to see the devastated look on his face, or see him pick up the ring and tuck it into his suitcase.

The throwing up started a few days later. I was to heartbroken to care. After a week of being sick in the morning and fine in the afternoon I did the math. My period was over a month late. I stepped into flip flops, which matched my whole bag lady appearance, and went to the drug store down the street...

CHAPTER 2

Sitting in the bathroom floor, head in my hands, freezing my ass off, I was scared to look at the test stick that was sitting on the sink. Rick had left almost three weeks ago, I'd been awake since then, I'd been crying since then, now I knew I'd probably start crying again as soon as I could stop being sick and work up the courage to look at the stupid test. "Okay you coward, either look at the stick and figure this crap out or sit here and let the tile freeze your ass." Talking to myself is something I've been working on lately. Apparently, I could motivate myself better than anyone. I reached up and took the stick off the sink. Opening one eye I looked at the two purple lines; then promptly threw up again. "Wonderful, just what I need; a baby!" (See what I mean about the talking to myself thing?) I sat on the floor in self-pity, or maybe it was self-loathing, for a few more minutes. Then stood up and looked myself in the eye. I shook my head to try to dislodge the fear I felt.

"Alright, time to make a few decisions here." After brushing my teeth and washing my face I went to my room and sat on the bed in silence trying to decide what to do. I was going to be a mother, that was a given, the only choice was to tell Rick or not. Well, there was always the option to sell everything I owned and run away to the beach and be a bum. Then I wouldn't have to tell anybody. He'd already moved on with whatever his mission was, he chose that life over a life with me. After that horrible day I had expected him to call, to apologize, something. I was even prepared to tell him I still loved him and would be here when he got back. But nothing, no calls, nothing. Allowing the anger to grow somehow made missing him a little easier so I went with it. "Screw him then! I can do this. The only question left to ask… am I kidding myself or am I just crazy. And I really need to stop talking to myself." I got up, took a hot shower threw away my sweat pants (yoga pants seemed much more pulled together) and headed for the kitchen. I started with the wine and ended with the processed cheese.

I put all the food in a box and left a note for my roommate

Christy "Get rid of this crap or I will eat it!" Then I called

my doctor to set up an appointment. (Better to get off on

the right foot.) Then I curled up on my bed and cried,

again.

That was how Christy found me when she got home

from work. She started talking as she came down the hall.

"Becca, are you okay? I saw the box in the kitchen are you

on a new health food kick or something?" I sat up and tried

to pretend everything was cool. I haven't been able to lie to

her since we met in the 10th grade. She sat on the bed

beside me and wrapped her arms around me. "Spill sister."

I couldn't help it, I started bawling like a little kid

with a broken heart. Between sobs I managed to get out

what had happened with Rick. "You don't need him

anyway, there are plenty of men out there who would jump

at the chance to be with you. But really, I think we should

keep the wine, might help with the whole healing thing."

I sat up and took a deep breath. "Christy, I'm pregnant." It took her all of 2 seconds before she started asking questions, was I going to tell Rick, could she kill him, what was wrong with him, that sort of thing. At the look on my face she stopped.

Gathering me in her arms again she said "We don't need that bastard anyway, I'll be the baby's daddy." Have you ever tried laughing and crying at the same time? It isn't pretty but that was the moment I started healing. I knew I wouldn't be alone after all.

A few days later I was finishing up my appointment. The doctor came back in the room once I was dressed again. "Well, you are pregnant alright. Judging by the look on your face you aren't exactly happy about it either." Dr. Kaspar had been my doctor since I was a kid, he didn't pull any punches, didn't sugar coat anything. He told it like it was. Usually I liked that about him, but this wasn't a broken rib or an ear infection. Right now, I needed the sugar coating. "You had to know this was a possibility. What about the father? Should I be expecting a wedding invitation anytime soon?" He wasn't being judgemental, just opinionated.

"It's not that I'm not happy, I'm just confused. The father is gone, he doesn't even know and I'm not telling him, I don't think. So, no wedding invitations, sorry. I wanted kids just not this early in life and certainly not by myself. I'm not sure I'm cut out to do the 'baby momma' thing."

"Well, you're healthy, and by the looks of things the baby will be too. Let me know when you have the shower, buying baby things for you may keep my wife from hounding our daughter about grandchildren." I sat in the doctor's waiting room for a few minutes before I could call Nita. "Hey Nita, I need to ask you a question. Have you heard from Rick since he left?"

"Jon is with his buddies in California for a few weeks but he called last night and asked me to go pack up Rick's apartment and put it all in storage. He's off somewhere he can't talk about, and he won't be back for a while. Why?"

I couldn't think for a moment. He was really gone for good. "So, he's still off saving the world?" I tried to sound like I didn't care, but I failed. "Oh well, no point in asking my next question then."

"Which was?"

"Should I let him know he's going to be a father or not? Since he already chose the mission over me once, I'm not going to give him a choice this time. You can't tell a soul by the way."

"Your secret is safe with me, but I can't speak for Jon, he and Rick have been friends since high school. Besides anyone who knows you will figure it out. Do you really want to do this alone?"

"It doesn't really matter if anyone knows, Jon is the only one who can get in touch with him, and I won't be alone, I have you guys, my parents and Christy."

"I'll be here for you anytime for anything you know that but that isn't the kind of alone I meant."

"I know but I really can't think about that right now, hey I better let you go. I've got to head over to mom and dad's. Not sure how they're going to take the news."

"Okay, love you girl."

I sat in the car for almost twenty minutes before I could start it and head to my parent's house. The drive seemed to take forever and yet when I got there I felt like I needed more time to prepare. I sat in the car across the street and looked at the little brick Tudor with the front porch swing and thought about growing up here. I was lucky, my parents were together about everything, if they did fight I never knew it. I had always imagined raising my children with a strong loving husband by my side.

Finally working up the balls to go inside I made the longest walk in history. Mom was making Sunday dinner and dad was watching the news so I started setting the table. "Not that I'm not grateful for the help but the only time you help in the kitchen is when you miss being a little girl, or you are buttering me up for something. Which is it?"

Smiling at my mother's normal blunt attitude, I decided to just spit it out. "Mom, I'm pregnant." My mom just looked at me for a moment as I looked at the floor, I could almost feel the disappointment.

"Okay, so should I ask about Rick or are we doing this without him?" Tears immediately sprung into my eyes, mom always knew how to get straight to the point. She gathered me in a tight embrace just as the tears started streaming down my cheeks. AGAIN! (Note to self; stop talking to myself AND stop crying all the time!) "So, it's just us then. It's ok, we'll figure it out. Now we just have to decide how to tell your dad."

The rest of the evening was spent having a nice dinner and avoiding discussing the baby. In his natural easy going way my father asked "Okay you two, what's up? You've been giving each other 'the look' all evening.

Mom and I looked at each other again. This was the real test right here. "Daddy, I'm pregnant. Rick is gone. He doesn't even know. Yes, I'm keeping the baby and no you can't kill Rick. Well on second thought if you can find him you can kill him." I just blurted it all out. I sat there and waited for the explosion. Dad looked at Mom. I remembered seeing that look many times. That was the 'what are we doing here' look. He was asking what mom wanted him to say to back her up. Always a united front.

Mom looked at me in what can only be described as sympathy-pity-pride. "We are going to be grandparents. Our daughter is having a baby and there is no greater blessing in our old age than grandchildren. Becca will be a great mom. If she just happens to be doing this without the father, then I say that's his loss." Dad grinned at her. He knew better than to argue when she had that look on her face.

He took a deep breath, "So will this kid be calling me something silly like 'paw paw' or do I get a vote?" I think Dad realized we had it under control and that we were taking this as happy news, so he decided to go along until Mom indicated he should do otherwise.

Having just finished my master's I decided this was as good a time as any to start my design business. I looked at so many buildings they all started to look alike. Then I found the one. It was actually an old bank. A really old bank. The decorative embellishments on the building were intact though and were completely amazing, between the pregnancy hormones and the luck of finding such a great place I spent a lot of time crying. I started renovating it, the upstairs became a two-bedroom apartment for myself and the little girl I was expecting; the downstairs became the office for my home decorating and design business. Christy handled the people end and the accounting and I did the actual design and decoration end. We decided to hire sexy cowboys when we needed heavy lifting done. (A perk of living in the country music capital, lots of sexy cowboys needing work while waiting to be discovered)

I loved being pregnant; feeling the baby kick, shopping for baby things, people giving me their taxis. (Especially the taxi part.) But I missed Rick every day. I started a thousand letters to him but threw them all away, they sounded lost and unhappy and I wasn't going to give him that satisfaction.

Then things started to fall apart; I went two days with no kicking, then four. I started to panic, I went to the doctor. They did so many tests I lost count. Mom came in and held my hand as the Dr. Kaspar gave me the news I had already started to expect. He told me the baby was gone. My little girl would be still born. They had no way of knowing what had caused her death. I sat; stunned; in his office, didn't cry or even blink. I think now that I had been in shock. He explained that I was too far along for a DNC, and I would need to deliver the baby and they wanted to induce labor as soon as possible. The day they started my labor I decided I wanted nothing more to do with Rick Dorsey. Ever.

After four hours of cursing Rick with my every breath I brought Lily Elizabeth into the world. Three days later I buried my daughter, and any love I still felt for Rick. That hatred would sustain me for a long time

CHAPTER 3

Christy left me to my grieving lonely existence for three years before the parade of dates started. That first year it was only one or two, but then it was one every couple of months, then once a month, then almost weekly she found some guy to set me up with. I had actually made several new friends that way. Had even helped a few of them meet the woman of their dreams. I was currently decorating the nursery of one of my blind dates first child. Christy was starting to run out of men thank God!

The latest was David. I had enjoyed dinner but David was not my type, no sense of adventure at all. He was a definite home body. He liked watching movies (think Star Trek) and conventions (yes comic book conventions, complete with costumes) Most of the night we talked about books, well that would have been fine, but we only talked about his book. He was writing a science fiction book about time travel. It really sounded good. I make him sound like a boring guy, and he wasn't. Really. Just felt like the conversation was forced, like we were searching for things to talk about. He was very nice, and after he relaxed a bit we had a pretty good time. By the time dinner was over the conversation was a bit broader and more interesting. We rode home continuing to chit chat.

I got out of the car when we pulled up. He walked me to the door. He suddenly looked very awkward, nervous even. I reached for his hand and he took it and visibly relaxed. "I had a nice time tonight David but I just think we'd make better friends than anything more. I'm sorry."

He literally breathed a sigh of relief. "I got the same feeling, you're a beautiful woman but the sparks just weren't there for either of us. I was so nervous about how to say that without hurting your feelings or coming off lame. But I had a good time. Maybe we can go out sometimes as friends? You know, a nice night out without all the romantic pressure might be a fun change."

"That actually sounds great, friends are hard to come by in this city. You have my number, give me a call sometime."

We hugged and David waited until I had gone inside and locked the door behind me before getting in his car and driving away. I bolted the door then headed upstairs to the apartment. Christy was standing at the top of the stairs waiting for me; hands on her hips.

"What was wrong with this one?" she got straight to the point, kind of like my mom come to think about it.

"Nothing wrong at all, just no sparks. We are going to go out again as just friends
sometime."

Her frustrated sigh followed me into the living room. "Okay, I give up. Jason was to wild, David not wild enough, and I forget what was wrong with the rest over the years. But I get the hint already, no more set ups."

I threw my hands in the air and did a white girl

version of the touchdown dance. "Finally! Seriously though, I just don't really want or need a man in my life right now, when the right man comes along I'll know it." Christy put her hand on my arm, "Rick isn't coming back, you know that. And until you let him go no one will compare to him."

I really hate it when she knows me better than I know myself. "I'm not comparing anyone to Rick. As a matter of fact, I haven't thought about him in so long I can barely remember the sound of his voice." At the look on her face I smiled softly, "okay, I'm lying, I can remember every detail about him; every scar, every look, everything. No man will ever be enough again, because my heart still belongs to him. But I'm okay with that, really, I am. I have my shop, Victoria and you, what more do I need in life?"

She smiled at me, "A lifetime supply of batteries!!" We both laughed pretty hard at that one. Mainly because it was true. Christy was in the same boat I was in as far as boyfriends went. BOB was a popular guy.

A cry from the living room made my smile go all the way to my eyes for the first time in hours. Heading to the crib I dropped my purse on the kitchen table and stepped out of my shoes. Victoria was only a few weeks old, her mother had been addicted to drugs and in an abusive relationship, she had made the decision to put the little angel up for adoption even before she was born. I had been on the list for almost two years when Victoria was born. Now she was mine. She was perfect, ten little toes, ten little fingers, she even had hair the same color as mine but her eyes were as bright a blue as they could be. Every time I held her my heart melted all over again. She was not a replacement for my lost angel, but she filled an empty space in my heart that I thought would never feel full again.

Later that night, after Victoria was in bed and Christy had gone home, I was just sinking into the pillows and drifting off when the phone rang.

"Hello?"

"Hi Becky." Well speak of the devil.

I almost dropped the phone. No one called me that except Rick. His voice was soft, deep and as sexy as I remembered. All the buried pain of the last four years hit me and it was all I could do to breath. That jolt of pain and recognition shot through my heart so fast I almost didn't answer. Struggling to regain my composure I finally spoke. "Rick, it's been a long time." I was obscenely proud that my voice didn't quiver.

"How are you?" His soft warm voice wrapped around me instantly, I forgot all the anger and the pain, almost.

"I'm fine. You?"

"Okay, just getting used to the weather here. It's much different this side of the world."

It took all of half a second for my brain to register his comment. "Here? Where are you this time?"

"I'm at Jon's. I'm looking for an apartment. That's how I got your number, well to be honest I had to steal your number from Nita's address book. Is it okay that I called you?"

He was here, not even an hour from where I was laying missing him? All the pain and sadness came rushing back. Suddenly I was very tired, disturbingly horny too, but mostly tired. "What do you want Rick? After almost four years of nothing, four years of living totally separate lives, why did you call?" I was a little surprised at the strength I heard in my own voice.

"I just want to see you. Don't hang up please. There are a few things I want the chance to explain to you. Stuff I didn't have the chance to say all those years ago."

I held my breath for a moment before answering him. What harm could come from one evening with an old... what? Lover, friend, love of a lifetime, soul mate? "Okay, but someplace we never went together, I don't want old memories drudged up now."

"Agreed, how about tomorrow night? I'll pick you up around seven and we'll go to the Spaghetti Factory."

"This isn't a date Rick; I'll meet you there at seven."

"I can agree with that. So what have you been up to since I left? Jon and Nita refuse to talk about you at all. I think they are protecting you from me or something."

We spent the next half hour just catching up on each other's lives. The conversation was slow, stilted. We were both pretending we were nothing more than old friends. I avoided saying what was most on my mind. I hoped he would broach the subject of our past, yet afraid of the conversation that would start.

"I better get to sleep now; I have a lot to do tomorrow."

"Okay. I can't wait to see you Becky." The timbre of his voice dropped and I could hear the husky tones I'd fallen in love with. "I've missed you."

I almost said the same words to him, but stopped myself just in time. "Goodnight Rick."

After I hung up the phone I went to my hope chest and pulled out the box with all the old mementos of our relationship. 'The Sap Box' Christy called it. I spent the rest of the night pathetically reading and re-reading them. (Don't judge, I said it was pathetic.)

When I did finally manage to fall asleep I dreamt of Rick riding in on a white horse and falling to his knees before me and begging my forgiveness for leaving and asking to be a family. I awoke exhausted and puffy eyed. It was going to be a beautiful day. NOT!

Rick

Hanging up the phone he released the breath he didn't even realize he'd been holding. She didn't hang up, that was something at least. The sound of her voice had made him remember all the nights he was alone in the dessert, the memories (some real and some imagined) were the only things that helped him hold on to what sanity he had managed to maintain. There were some nights he wanted to just stop fighting and die, but the image of her face kept rising in front of him and forcing him to live, and finally to try to escape.

Tossing the phone on the recliner he dropped down on the couch and tried to convince himself she had really said yes. Maybe this was a bad idea. What if she just laughed at him and told him to fuck off? God only knew he deserved it. Worse yet, what if she was married, happily? All he really wanted was a chance to tell her he was sorry and that he wanted to be with her. He wasn't sure why he wanted to apologize. Oh, he understood he had been an ass and she deserved an apology, but he had never felt the need to say the words 'I'm sorry'. He reached into his briefcase and pulled out his laptop. He looked up the nightlife of Nashville and tried to think of things they could do that would be romantic but not too much too soon. If he were honest with himself, he would admit that he didn't care if they ate hotdogs on the street corner as long as they did it together. Noting the times of the carriage rides by the river, he let himself picture sitting in the carriage with her smiling up at him as he wrapped his arms around her.

He pulled up the website for her business and looked at the pictures of her. There were some where she was wearing dressy clothes and looking very professional, but his favorite were the ones showing her 'hands on', blue jean shorts and t-shirt; covered in paint with the biggest sexiest smile he had seen in years. He felt his cock stirring in his pants, seeing her always made his body react that way. Closing the computer, he headed for the shower. Stripping quickly, he stepped into the shower. The hot water felt amazing as it hit his already over heated skin, closing his eyes he ran his hand down his chest trying to convince himself not to jack off to her memory again. It was no use he couldn't avoid it any more than he could avoid breathing. In his mind she was in the shower with him, her hand gripping his cock gently and stroking it just the way she knew he loved it, starting at the base with a feather touch and growing tighter and firmer as she pulled toward the end of his shaft. The hot water and soap bubbles on his hand became her pussy, slippery wet and tight on his cock. His breathing deepened and he lifted onto his toes as his body started to tremble, his cum exploded all over his hand and into the bottom of the shower. He leaned against the wall to regain his composure. At least a little of the tension was gone from his body, until he saw her again on Saturday of course. He knew he would have a hard cock from the moment he caught site of her until she told him she never wanted to see him again.

Leaving the shower, he slipped on a robe and walked the perimeter of Jon's apartment double checking the doors and windows one last time, then he used his laptop to check the cameras he had placed outside her doors. Both appeared secure and the street was empty. Convinced she wasn't being watched yet he went to bed.

CHAPTER 4

Becca

Dawn came entirely too early, but I got Tori to Mom's on time and got back to the office in time for coffee with Christy before my first client of the morning.

We were sitting at the table going over some notes, I really had no idea how to start the conversation so I decided to just jump in. "You'll never guess who I got a call from after you left last night."

"Who?"

"Rick." Christy sat her coffee cup down and just looked at me. Said nothing. Just sat there and stared at me. "He is in town for a few days and wants to have dinner." Still no words, just staring, only difference is now her left eyebrow was arched. "Says he wants to apologize and explain why he left. I said yes. I'm meeting him tonight."

"You're doing what?" Christy was livid. "Are you nuts? That schmuck broke your heart and you still aren't really over him and now you are going on a date? You literally cried for years over that idiot! Why would you even consider seeing him again?"

"Christy, it isn't a date. Just two old friends, and we are just going to dinner. No big deal! Will you watch Tory please?"

"Of course I will. But when he breaks your heart again, which he will, I reserve the right to say 'I told you so' until the cows come home, and don't you dare come crying to me." She got up and stormed off to her office, then ruined it by having to come back for her coffee, but the effect was the same, she was mad. Really mad. I hollered "Deal" down the hall after her. I saw no point in arguing, she would say it anyway. And if he did break my heart again I knew she would be there to pick up the pieces again, just like last time. I spent the rest of the day trying to work on various projects.

My first client was a newlywed couple who had just

bought an old building downtown and wanted me to completely gut and renovate it. The pictures they had showed me 12 foot ceilings, complete with crown molding and original chandeliers. There were rooms upstairs they wanted to turn into 3 bedrooms and 2 bathrooms, the layout was going to be amazing. Even with all that was going on I was totally excited about this project. We spent an hour talking about what they wanted from the space. When they left we had a handshake deal in place and I would have a contract to them in 2 days. I wanted to be in the house by the end of the week with sketch pad and camera.

The second client was an office remodel for a lawyer who had just made partner, he looked to be in his early 50's, especially sitting next to his 'personal assistant' who didn't look a day over 21, basically he was willing to over pay (a lot) so I would pick out his new furniture rather than pass the job to his new secretary (who was surprisingly attentive to the level of 'plush' in the new furniture during the meeting). I agreed to take the job, based on the pictures he brought me it would be a simple matter of picking out the new stuff then finding the best arrangement for his 'needs'. Easy money. A lot of easy money.

Client number three was tall, very handsome in clean cut preppy sort of way. Black hair, eyes so dark I couldn't tell if they were black or brown, moustache, tall and thin. He wore black slacks and a black button up shirt under a leather jacket. He had an accent too, not British, not German; but it was obvious his accent was forced. I had to make myself maintain my professionalism during the meeting.

He told me about a farm house about an hour from downtown and wanted to turn it into a bed and breakfast. While he talked, he walked, actually almost paced around the room while we were talking and kept stopping to ask questions about the pictures I had hanging up. Mostly project pictures but the ones on my desk were Tori, Mom and Dad. I kinda got the creeps from him and decided to call him later and turn down the project. I wouldn't mind the money but he seemed stalker-ish to me.

He gave me the blueprints for the house which was odd but not as odd as the butt of the gun that was momentarily visible as he leaned forward to hand me the paper. I don't know a lot about guns but I recognized the .45 caliber pistol. He noticed my reaction to the gun and leaned back quickly and pulled his jacket closed. I was definitely going to call and cancel this job. No amount of money was worth putting up with the vibe I was getting from this guy.

At about 5 o'clock I stepped into the shower and started getting ready for the evening. The hot water felt so good, I tried to pretend it wasn't the thought of Rick that made my hands move slowly over my body. I imagined his hands touching me. Sliding my fingers along the lips of my pussy felt so wonderful, I leaned against the wall of the shower and found my clit with one hand while I used the other to pinch my erect nipples. It only took a few minutes of thinking of him and I was cumming in spasms more powerful than any I'd given myself in years.

Finishing the actual 'cleaning' part of the shower quickly I hurried to get ready to see him. I was proud of my figure and wanted to show it off, okay to be honest I wanted Rick to know exactly what he had walked away from. After putting perfume in all the right places, I picked out a pale pink lace bra and panty set that looked fabulous against my skin. I let my little black dress slide into place. At first my hair fell to my waist in soft curls, then I thought again, remembering how much he had liked to play with my hair I pulled the whole mass into a loose bun with wispy bangs. I left the hose in the package and slipped into the sexy black heels I'd had to literally dig out of the back of the closet. Taking one last look in the mirror I was satisfied he would want me still. (Although I wasn't sure why that mattered.) Maybe even then I had plans to use him like I felt he had used me. I picked up my purse and left for downtown.

He was waiting by the front door of the restaurant when I arrived at quarter to seven. I sat in the car and looked at him for a few minutes. Years ago, he would have been casually leaned up against the wall, tonight he seemed almost wired. His muscles were tense and he scanned the crowd as if looking for someone. I noticed but all I could think about was how he looked so sexy in his typical black slacks and black polo shirt. His hair was short like always but I remembered just how soft and thick it was. My fingers itched to touch it again. He kissed my cheek when I reached his side and his lips left a heat that tingled with remembered passion. "You look amazing Becky." He was looking at me like a starving man looked at food.

"Thank you, you look very nice too." I noticed the

small scar across the bridge of his nose that hadn't been there before. I wanted so much to reach out and touch it but I didn't. I wanted to wrap my arms around him and hold him close, but I didn't. Hell, I wanted to slap him for all the pain he had caused, but the whole 'mature adult' part of my brain took over and told my heart to shut up.

Dinner went fine, we talked about friends we used to have in common, "I take it you've been staying with Jon and Nita?"

"Yes, I've found an apartment now though so I'll be moving out in the next day or so. Do you still talk to them often?"

"Almost every day. Nita is one of my best friends. I'm actually surprised she let you stay with them. Jon has been a great help to me since I bought the building down town. He does everything on my 'honey-do' list. He taught me how to shoot, I'm pretty good. What have you been up to? I assumed you had either settled down or taken over an island somewhere."

He starred at me for a moment like he wanted to say something. He looked down at his napkin before speaking. It was his comment of 'not much' that took the last ounce of my polite reserve. Suddenly I was so totally pissed at him I could barely breathe. "Rick, you said you have something specific you wanted to explain to me. What is it?"

He took a deep breath and a long swallow of his wine. "Four years ago, when I left, it was to go on one last assignment. I knew I would be gone for several years but there was no way I could know how long for sure. I wanted to let you know how much I loved you and that it would be my last trip but I couldn't ask you to wait for me when I didn't even know if I would be coming back."

I felt as if I had been punched, my stomach was doing flips and my heart literally ached. "When you left you told me you couldn't choose me over that life. If you knew it was your last mission, why didn't you tell me that and let me decide if I wanted to wait or not? I thought you just loved the danger more than you loved me. All these years I thought you had rejected me. Why did you have to lie?" It was all I could do to hold back the tears, but I would rather die than have him see me cry over him. (There would be time for that later.)

He reached for my hand across the table. I felt the slight tremor in his hand and was glad he was just as affected by this situation as I was. "No I never said I couldn't choose you. You never let me say anything baby. You walked out."

"You hesitated, that told me exactly what you thought. The words never came out of your mouth, but actions spoke volumes."

Rick

He didn't know how to respond. He'd expected anger or even tears, but her straight forward questions with the pain he saw in her eyes, barely visible but there just the same, it was almost too much for him. "I wanted you to hate me. I thought that if you hated me it would be easier for you because you wouldn't want me back and easier for me because I would know you no longer wanted me in your life."

She stared at her hands in his for a long moment. When she spoke it was so soft, he almost didn't hear her. What she said almost killed him.

"It didn't work you know. The hating you part; for a while I did hate you, but after a few weeks I wanted you more than I ever had. It was almost three years before I went on a date."

Her honesty surprised him. Maybe he had expected her to say how easy it was to move on. "I'm sorry, I never meant to hurt you." He continued to hold her clasped hands in his. "I dreamt of you every night. Sometimes thinking of you in my arms was the only reason I made it through the night at all. I started a million letters to you in my head but nothing sounded right. If I could go back; there are so many things I would do differently." He forced himself to stop there, it wouldn't have been fair to tell her the things he went through. The pain, the torture. He wanted to spare her any pain possible.

"Where were you Rick? What was so important it kept you away for so many years?"

He almost told her. He wanted to tell her, wanted her to understand. The mission, the betrayal, the capture, the escape, the ongoing danger, all of it. But if he told her the things he'd done; she would leave him sitting there alone. He knew that if he was alone again it would be forever this time. He'd spent enough time alone to last a life time.

He decided to tell her enough to make her understand it wasn't by his choice that he was away from her. Taking a deep breath, he just started talking. "I was in a little camp in northern Afghanistan for over a year. At first, we were trying to infiltrate the group to get info then when we realized the horrors they were enacting on the locals we got the info we needed and turned on them to help the people. We were captured" his voice was shaking and he paused to pull himself together, "out of eight men only four lived long enough to escape, four years. It took us another few months to reach an American military base. Then back here to try to regain some semblance of a normal life." He saw the fear and the pity on her face and hated himself for contacting her, he should have just left her alone to get on with her life. He started to pull his hands away from hers, she took his hands and held them, the protective gesture gave him a moment of hope. "I'm sorry Becky, I shouldn't be telling you any of this. I'm just trying to say that I didn't stay gone out of any choice of my own."

"The scar on your nose? How did you get that? Were you hurt bad?"

He played down the pain to protect her. "I was shot in the shoulder and fell through a sliding glass door. It didn't hurt as bad as you would think."

Becca

In my mind's eye I saw every POW camp I'd ever seen in movies. I pictured the man I loved in a tiny cage in some desert thinking I hated him. I suddenly couldn't breathe. I downed the rest of my wine and put the glass on the table. Thinking of him in danger, probably in pain was too much for me. "Alright, this conversation is a little more than I can deal with right now. Let's go for a walk so I can clear my head." Nodding, he called for the check and I headed outside into the cool night air. Taking a deep breath, I let it fill my lungs.

We decided to walk the few blocks to the river. There were several horse carriages ready to take people on the scenic view of old downtown. We rode in silence for a few minutes, both lost in thoughts of the years we had been apart. Then the carriage hit a bump in the road and we both jumped. He put his arm around me to help me balance. The contact sent chills up my spine but I didn't object, so he left his arm around my shoulders. Deciding to enjoy the warmth he represented I scooted closer to him. Our bodies were touching from hip to knee. He pointed out sites he didn't remember and I played tour guide filling him in on the details of when things were added. It was all I could do to pay attention to the conversation, the heat from his arm seemed to have a direct effect on the heat moving through my body. After the ride, we walked back toward the cars and he reached for my hand. I let his large work roughened fingers entwine with my much smaller ones, his hands were huge and tan just like the rest of him but I had always loved his hands, so strong. I noticed a small scar on the back of his left hand that hadn't been there before. Touching it with one finger I went for levity. "Please tell me you didn't get shot in the hand."

He sort of grinned at my poor attempt at humor. "No, actually that is a fairly new scar. I let a drunk idiot get to close to me with a knife." Anyway, we walked the rest of the way back in silence. Both lost in our own thoughts of what the night's conversation had meant. I wasn't sure what the future may bring but I let myself pretend for this one night.

We said goodnight at my car and hugged briefly. I felt his lips on my neck as he placed a small kiss on the spot that used to drive me wild. I closed my eyes and moaned without thinking about it. I melted. Right there on the street, with the man who had shattered my world. His tongue ran in quick circles and he gently nipped at the nerve where my neck became shoulder. I grabbed his arms and even I wasn't sure if I was pushing him away or pulling him closer. Maybe I was just holding on for dear life! He leaned back and looked into my eyes. We both wanted more, but I wasn't going to venture that far, and he didn't push. I stepped back from his embrace and said goodnight again. Then I got in the car and started it. I didn't look at him again, afraid I would make another mistake and ask him to spend the night with me. As it was I knew I would spend the night dreaming about him. I realized then that his world had been just as shattered as mine had. The rest of my anger melted in that moment.

CHAPTER 5

The next morning, I sat in my office telling Christy all about the evening. Well, not about the touching parts! "Do you think he really wants a relationship or is he just trying to get some while he's in town?"

"Christine Lyons! My God! Sometimes your mouth amazes even me! But you do ask a good question, I don't know what he wants but I wouldn't mind 'getting some' while he's in town." I wiggled my eyebrows; going for levity!

"Becca, do you really want to let him get that close?" Apparently, she wanted to stay serious.

"I'm not talking about starting a relationship with him, just some 'no strings attached' type fun is all. It's been almost four years you know! I wonder if I'm a virgin again?" I laughed out loud but I really was thinking about fucking Rick. He was the only man I'd ever had, and the things he had made me feel still haunted my dreams at night. Over the years, I had managed to keep myself from going crazy but even his face in my mind and my fingers on my clit were a poor substitute for his body over mine.

"At the risk of sounding corny, what about the strings attached to your heart? Do you really want to put them back in his hands?"

"Wow, that was corny. Again, with the good questions. I don't really know what I want at this point. But for now I have work to do, I promised Mrs. Whitman we'd be over this week to finish picking the colors for her sitting room." She looked away from me. "Chris, I know you are worried about me but I will be okay. I promise I won't do anything without thinking about the consequences first."

Christy sighed, "Just don't let him hurt you again." She allowed the subject to change at this point. "I'm still trying to decipher her notes from the last order form from her dining room. I appreciate her business but maybe you should let her dictate and you write down what she wants?"

I tried to concentrate on Mrs. Whitman's living room, I really did, but my mind kept drifting back to the man I'd had dinner with last night. He had truly been my whole world, I had lived and breathed for him. Then he destroyed me. Broke my heart so badly I still hadn't recovered. To be perfectly honest, I wasn't sure I ever would.

Now what? He's out of the service and he wants to be a part of my life again? Mentally hiking myself back to the present I decided to let the future worry about itself for a change. This time I was going to do what I wanted to do instead of the 'right' thing. It had been years since I'd had sex (with anyone other than myself.) It was time to change that!!! I made a concerted effort to get some work done, between the fabric swatches and the purchase orders I lost track of the Whitman file. "Christy, did I leave Mrs. Whitman's file out there? I can't remember which green she wanted for the sofa."

The door to my office opened. "How many shades of green can there be?" The deep resonating voice made my insides flutter. Rick smiled at me when I looked up at him. "Hi."

I'd spent most of last night dreaming of that voice, oh who the hell was I trying to kid; I'd spent most of the last four years dreaming of him. "Christy just stepped out, something about a new gallery downtown. I don't think she likes me at all now. She probably wanted to throw me out, but I brought us lunch and she seemed ok with me feeding you. Do you have a break room or something?"

"Lunch? I thought you had business to handle today?" I was surprised I didn't just throw him out, (or maybe jump him where he stood.)

"I finished my stuff early so we could have lunch." He looked so delicious I knew what I wanted to eat.

I just looked at him for a few minutes. "Okay, well I

don't have a break room but I live upstairs, we can eat up there." I walked past him to lock the front door then led the way upstairs. "Christy said she was going to a new gallery? Well we won't see her for a while." Trying not to think about what I wanted to do with those few hours I was keenly aware that Rick was watching my ass as I led him upstairs. I opened the door to my apartment and when he walked in he seemed surprised that it didn't look like the upstairs of a warehouse.

"This is amazing; I assume you decorated it yourself." He walked around and took in the homey atmosphere of the converted rooms, the furniture was light colored and placed to give as much open space as possible. A beautiful antique lowboy stood against one wall covered in framed photos.

"Yes, as soon as I bought the building, business really took off. I spent so much time here that it made more sense to stay here than to drive back and forth every day. And Tori will have plenty of room to grow." As soon as my daughter's name came out of my mouth I froze, he didn't know about any of it, Lily, her death or Tori.

"Is this your daughter?" He was looking at the pictures I had so many of.

"Yes, that was taken the day I brought her home." I wanted to say more, tell him everything to be exact but I didn't quite trust him yet.

I could see the struggle in his face, I only hoped he hadn't become one of those men who hated kids or anything. "Do you mind if I ask where her father is?"

"I think he is in jail by now." Rick turned at my pause and rose an eyebrow in question.

I considered letting him think I had moved on, but I never could lie very well. "She is adopted Rick. Her birth mother was abused and did drugs, she wanted a better life for her baby girl. I'm going to give it to her."

"She's a beautiful little girl." Was that relief on his face? Before I had much time to ponder his expression he broke the spell. "Now point me in the direction of the

kitchen and I'll set this out while you go wash up."

Rick

As he watched Becca head toward her bathroom his eyes drifted back to the picture of her holding the little girl in her arms. While he was in Afghanistan the thought of being with her and starting a family had been his 'happy place', here she was, single with a built-in family. He had been having second thoughts about pursuing Becca simply because he didn't want to risk being the reason that little girl didn't have her real father. He thought the father was still in their lives and that he was a lover of Becca's. Knowing that the baby was adopted by Becca alone and that the birth parents were out of the picture made his decision to continue working his way into her life for as long as he could much easier to maintain. This way he only had old guilt to deal with not new guilt. Saying a silent prayer that he could maybe become a permanent fixture in both their lives he headed to the kitchen.

Becca

In the bathroom with the door safely closed I looked at my reflection in the mirror and spoke softly. "What the hell are you doing? You put Rick Dorsey behind you years ago. Why are you letting him back in now? Just when you can breathe without pain. So, he can break your heart again? Will it really be worth it to feel like death again just to spend a few nights in his arms?"

Knowing I would regret it forever if I let him walk away without touching him; without loving him one more time, I came to a decision, or maybe it was just a lie I could almost believe. "Okay, he'll only be here for a few days then he'll go back to wherever he's been and out of my life for at least another four years. I can do this!" Taking one more deep breath I opened the door and stepped into the hallway. The smell of cooking food beckoned me. The sight in my little kitchen made me smile, Rick stood at the stove with my apron tied around his lean hips and a towel tossed over one muscled shoulder. I looked past him to the dining room table. It was covered with all the normal picnic food, only with a twist. The salad boasted almonds and cranberries, the mac and cheese was topped with a golden-brown layer of cracker crumbs. The wine was in real glasses, not the plastic ones you normally took on a picnic. "Oh wow, it looks like you've made a feast."

He turned and smiled at me. From the fire in his eyes I got the feeling he wanted to feast on something other than food and I fully intended to let him. "I set the table, go sit down, I'm trying to capture a mood here."

Laughing, I went to the table and sat in awe of the candles and the flowers. "What else do you have in that magic bag?"

"Nothing much now." He sat the honey glazed pork chops on the table and sat down. We made small talk for a while. It was as if we were getting to know each other all over again. By some unspoken agreement, we stayed away from mention of the past and concentrated on the present, maybe even pretended there might be a future. "Tell me about your business, is it what you expected when you started it?"

"Actually, it is. I get to take apart someone else's whole design concept, shop with someone else's money and decorate someone else's space and get paid very well to do it."

"What kind of people do you usually work for? I would think it would be mostly business offices with as close to downtown as you are."

"Well I do get a lot of 'office remodels' but there are several new townhome complexes going up all over Nashville, I get the contract on several of those a month. But sometimes I get the chance to do something wonderful. There is an old farm just outside of the county, it has this amazing two story home with amazing charm and details, the last owner put in a complete basement with several rooms as well. I'm dying to get that job, but the owner really gives me the creeps so I'm going to turn it down. But I would give my eye teeth to redo that building."

"What's so creepy about the guy that you would walk away from it.?"

"Just the way he walked around my office during out meeting, looking at all my pictures, asking personal questions. Seemed very odd to me." I was just about to tell him about the gun on the creepy owner when the phone interrupted us and I got up to answer it. "Yes?"

"Since when do you bolt the door from the inside during the day? I can't get in. If you're telling me to take the rest of the day off that's fine but I need some files from my desk to take home."

"Christy, what are you doing back so soon?" I tried to hide the disappointment I felt at her interruption.

"Soon? I've been gone for three hours! What have you two been up to since I left?"

"Very funny! I'll be right down." I hung up the phone and turned to Rick. "This was wonderful but I do need to get back to work."

"You go let her in and I'll finish up here then meet you downstairs."

I wasn't quite ready to say goodbye yet. "I'll open the door then come back up to help with the dishes." I fairly flew down the stairs and opened the door. "I'm sorry. I had no idea it was so late. Thank you for not sending him away. Why didn't you tell him we didn't have a break room? Never mind; you knew I'd have to take him upstairs. That's why."

Christy just smiled. "You're welcome. Now go back upstairs and finish whatever I interrupted. The sooner you get it out of your system the sooner this debacle will be over." She laughed as I took the stairs two at a time. I didn't care that she knew I was anxious to get back to him. As I stepped into the apartment

I heard the dishwasher close. Rick was washing the last pot at the sink. "You cook, you do dishes, is there anything you can't do?"

Rick looked at me for a moment; it was obvious he wanted to say much more. "Well, I can't get this apron untied, my hands are all wet."

I stepped behind him to undo the knot. My fingers brushed against his back and my heart raced. As soon as I released the knot and started to step back he turned around and pulled me toward him. "And I can't resist the beauty of your lips, can I kiss you?" I stared at his mouth and nodded. He lowered his lips to mine and softly caressed them. His tongue lightly brushed my lips and I parted them in invitation. He explored my mouth with his tongue and pulled me closer against his body. I let my hands run across his chest, I could feel the muscles through his shirt. His heat made me shiver in anticipation. I moved my hands over his shoulders to wrap my arms around his neck and pull him closer still. I melted against him and his arousal was evident against my belly. He ended the kiss, but kept me close to him. "God, I've missed you."

"I've missed you too. Nobody ever kissed me the way you did." My voice was soft and husky, dragged from a throat that was too dry, too tight to speak naturally. I swallowed hard and slicked a moist pink tongue over suddenly parched lips, watching his black gaze drop just for a moment to follow the tiny revealing gesture. When his eyes lifted again, burning straight into mine, I knew I was lost. No matter how angry or hurt I felt, there was just something about him that called out to my soul, always had been. I had fallen into sensual slavery without knowing why or how it had happened. But I was in and tumbling head over heels into an endless chasm of awareness, one from which I already knew I had no hope of escape.

Not that I wanted to, that smile had rocked my world, it had only been a small curl at the corners of his sexy mouth, but it had made me shiver in instant reaction, heated pinpricks of awareness tormenting my sensitized flesh. Despite the heat of the day I was shivering as if a cold draft had blown over my heated skin. Having looked into the dark depths of his eyes, I found I couldn't look away but was held captive. I knew the saving grace of all my years of anger was deserting me, evaporating in the warmth of his smile. When I saw the faint golden glow of amusement which lit those amazing eyes then I was lost. All the resistance in me melted like ice before a fire. He could sense my acceptance.

"Becky..." he whispered and the heat of his breath brushed along my cheek, stirring a tendril of hair at the lobe of my ear.

"Kiss me Rick." I begged him. The warmth of his mouth covered mine, his tongue teased my bottom lip then slipped inside again. Without ending the kiss, I started backing toward the living room. He must have known what

I was doing because he picked me up and moved us quickly to the couch, laying me down he started to lay over me, I pushed him back so I could see his eyes. I whispered, "take off your shirt, I need to feel your skin against mine." I pulled my shirt and bra off and tossed them aside and joined our lips again as he unbuttoned his shirt. Before he could get it off all the way I flexed my hands against the hard expanse of his chest. I felt ridges there that hadn't been there before, opening my eyes I saw the scars that criss crossed his chest, I pushed the material off his shoulders and down his arms, more scars, they were everywhere. He had stopped moving, bracing himself above me he was watching my face. I lifted my eyes to meet his.

Instead of the pity most would feel, all I could think was how proud I was that this man had gone through so much and had come home looking for me. "Sometime I want to know about these." I ran my hands up his chest and behind his neck, pulling him down to meet my lips. He sat up and reached for his belt I couldn't wait to see all of him. He grabbed my wrists with one hand and pulled me against him as we rolled from the couch onto the soft carpet of my living room floor. His lips claimed mine again in a fevered kiss as he opened his pants and only released me long enough to slide them off, leaving him sitting naked before me.

He reached for me again only I pushed him back onto the carpet and stretched out beside him so I could trail sweet kisses down his body, I avoided the scars not wanting to hurt him, his hands gently stroked across my shoulders. "You don't have to be afraid of them."

I looked at his eyes, "I'm not afraid of the scars, I'm afraid I'll hurt you. Aren't they painful?"

"No, they don't hurt anymore. They're just a little bit more sensitive than the rest of my skin. You won't hurt me."

I took a split second to absorb that information. 'a little more sensitive' huh? Time to see how sensitive. I bit and sucked on his nipples and smiled when I heard his responding hiss of pleasurable pain. Letting my hand roam toward his shoulder, I gently traced the scar there with my finger, then I placed butterfly kisses on the flesh, finally I ran my tongue over the scar tissue. His manhood, already at attention, began to pulse. I moved lower, tracing the chiseled contours of his abs with my tongue. He growled his enthusiasm as my soft fluttering kisses move down his shaft. He moaned my name as those kisses come back up his cock and they weren't so soft anymore. Each touch getting hotter and firmer. I moved back up to the tip, not kissing anymore but licking, sucking. He grabbed my shoulders and pulled me on top of him then rolled so I was beneath his body.

"You were the last woman I touched. If we don't slow down I won't be able to control myself. It'll be hot and hard and probably rougher than you can handle, and I don't want to hurt you."

"You're the only man I've ever touched and I've been a long time without you, I want you inside me." The contact of his chest against my nipples made me gasp as I added "so hot, hard and rougher than you think I can handle is exactly what I want." My body lifted away from the carpet as he pushed my skirt down my legs and tossed it toward the pile of clothes mingling against the wall. He looked at my panties and shook his head,

"These are in my way." He tore the flimsy material from my body and threw it away from us. Then he wasted no time in putting his hand between my thighs and pushing one finger, then two, deep into my throbbing wet pussy, while his thumb started a maddening assault on my clit that had me convulsing in pre-climax shudders.

"My god, you are tighter than I remembered." His voice is thick with hunger. "I'm burning to be inside you. Is that where you want me? Is that where you need me? I need to hear you say it baby."

I reached for his hips and tried to pull him toward me. "Yes, Rick! Please, now" Before I uttered another word he pushed my knees apart and settled his length against my pussy and drove deep inside me. I held onto his arms and met him thrust for glorious thrust. I started to cum, I tightened like a vice around his cock, my orgasm sending us both completely over the edge. He growled, deep and low and guttural, a primitive sound that filled my senses as completely as he filled my body. Pumping in and pulling out, he held my legs as he thrust harder and harder, the pain and pleasure coming together as one as my body tightened again, the spiraling desire building and building, so that only that place where his body penetrated mine existed. He came, hard, his body convulsing fiercely through his release. Our bodies shuddered together and he hugged me to him until the tremors stopped. He rolled on his back, carrying me with him, then he smiled. "That wasn't how I saw this date going. But you have this effect on me. I wanted to be gentle and tender the first time."

I laughed softly, "maybe next time." We laid there together for a while. I wanted him to go so I could think, but I didn't want to let go of him. Eventually I sat up and started reaching for my clothes.

"I have a few things to wrap up today. Can I call you later?"

I thought for a split second, really, I did. My heart answered before my brain could stop me. "Sure." I was trying for nonchalance, I think it worked.

He got dressed, picked up his bag and we headed for the door. I followed him down the stairs; he had a sexy ass. He stopped and pulled me against him for a kiss. Just that quickly I was ready for him again. We stepped apart and grinned at each other. We said goodbye at the door and I watched through the glass as his car pulled away.

"Sooo, how was lunch?" Christy could see my face and the heat I still felt on my skin, she knew exactly how 'lunch' went.

"Fine." I smiled at her.

"Did you tell him about her?" Whoa! Buzz kill.

I feigned ignorance. "What about her, he already knows I have a daughter."

"Yes, but does he know HE had a daughter?"

"He doesn't need to know. In a few days he'll go back to work and forget all about me. So, what difference does it make?" I cringed at Christy' exasperated look. "I'm going to go make a few calls then take a shower."

I never did get that shower, between the calls from customers and my mind drifting off I was still at my desk when it was time to go get Tori from day care. We had dinner and at 6 o'clock my freshly bathed angel was tucked into her crib. I relaxed in the giant tub. It had been my one concession to luxury when I designed the upper floor as an apartment. Just as I started to drift off the phone rang.

"Damn!" The handset was sitting on the edge of the sink. It rang again. Hopeful that I knew who it was I got out of the tub and padded naked across the room to answer it. "Hello?"

"Hi Becky, this is Rick. I'm sorry it's so late. Did I wake you?"

"No, just relaxing in the tub." I stepped back into the water and let the warmth soak back into my body. "What are you up to?"

I heard him take a deep breath and knew he was thinking of me naked. "Actually, I just got back to Jon's house. It's been a long afternoon of meetings today. What I was calling about was dinner, are you free Saturday about seven?"

I tried to think of a reason I couldn't go; really, I did, but Tori was spending the weekend with her grandparents; so, there was no excuse. "Sure, sounds great.

What did you have in mind?"

I let him tell me his plans because if I told him what was on my mind I'd end up asking him to come over right then. He went on about dinner plans. "I was thinking something relaxing. Do you still like pizza?"

"Sure pizza is fine."

"Okay, I'll pick up some movies and pizza and we can come back here. I don't think my apartment will be comfortable since I won't have furniture yet."

I took a bracing breath and jumped with both feet, "Why don't you just come here? It's a long drive to Jon's. Besides here we can put our feet on the sofa."

"That will work. So, seven o'clock at your place. Now, are you really in the tub?"

I laughed and then splashed the water a little so he could hear it. "Yep, all alone in this great big tub."

Rick groaned, "If I were there would you let me in the tub with you?"

I may have thought about it for a few split seconds. "Yes." Guess he noticed the playful quality was gone from my voice.

"You would?"

"Rick, I know you won't be here long, but I like how you make me feel. I'm willing to risk a few tears later for a lot of pleasure now." I waited for a minute but Rick didn't say anything. "Did I scare you away?"

"Not scared, just not sure what to say. Except that we better end this phone call now or I won't be able to walk across the room."

I smiled to myself, it was nice to know I could still have that effect on him. Especially since all he had to do was smile at me and I was hot and wet instantly. "Okay see you Saturday at seven."

"It's a date. Sleep well."

Rick

He tried to think about the fact that Becca was willing to spend time with him even though she didn't trust him and expected him to hurt her. But it wasn't the head on his shoulders that was in charge. He kept remembering how soft she was, and the way she smelled. The thought of her naked in the bathtub made his cock hard. Walking across the room to the mini bar, he tried to ignore the tightness in his boxers. As the scotch burned its way down his throat he realized he didn't want to ignore the heat Becca sent coursing thru his body. Laying on his back on the bed he let his hand move inside the material covering his cock. It was throbbing with his desire to be inside her. As he closed his eyes his hand became her pussy, hot and tight, moving slowly up and down the shaft of his rock-hard cock. The feeling intensified, he came in hot spurts. Laying there with his cum running down the back of his hand he smiled. "It's a date huh? I wonder how permanent a date it could be."

Becca

We said goodnight and hung up the phone. I leaned back against the tub. "What is wrong with me? I must secretly enjoy the feeling of a broken heart." I knew I wanted to feel the thrills Rick's hands could bring, I wanted to be held and made love to, and I can admit it, I wanted some just plain fucking too. When I had told Rick it had been a long time I hadn't been exaggerating. The last man who had touched me (before today) had been Rick himself. I had gone on several dates over the years but never more than once or twice with the same man. I generally spent the entire night comparing the poor guy to Rick anyway. Then coming home and fingering myself into oblivion. Didn't feel anywhere near as wonderful as the real thing but it was better than starting a relationship I knew wouldn't work. "Guess I'll just wait and see what happens."

Getting out of the tub and ready for bed took twice as long because I kept stopping and thinking about him. Thinking about Rick and what I wanted to happen made me tingle all over. As I was rubbing lotion on my skin I pretended my fingers were his fingers and started rubbing my body. Eventually I let my fingers slide over my clit, as they started circling that magic little button my breathing grew ragged until stars exploded behind my eyes. I had big plans for Saturday night and I fell asleep with a wicked smile on my face.

CHAPTER 6

The rest of the week flew by. Christy and I spent
most of the time finishing the decorating on Mrs.
Whitman's town house. First we took out the furniture that
was only a few years old, had it delivered to the local
nondenominational church, then brought in the new cream
colored chairs and chaise, finally the sage green sofa was
brought in. I had to smile every time I looked at that green
sofa. Rick was right; the color did seem out of place with
the classy furniture occupying the rest of the house, but I
had to admit that sitting next to the cream of the rest of this
room the sage wasn't so bad. Funny, but the first thought I
had was to tell Rick.

Later that afternoon I dropped off my sketches for
the townhouse job and called 'creepy guy' to decline the
job. The number was disconnected, thinking I had dialed it
wrong I called it again, same result. Disconnected. Oh well,

one less awkward conversation I had to have.

Saturday morning, I met the grandparents for breakfast at the local pancake house. I thought about telling them about Rick being back in town but I was pretty sure Dad still wanted to kill him so I decided against it. After listening to them dote on their new grand-daughter I headed to the mall to pick up something special for the night.

Ten minutes to seven I was standing in front of the full length mirror. First, I made sure the short skirt was laying right and the white shirt was neatly tucked in. I left my hair down and my auburn curls reached almost to my waist. "Okay, I got myself into this situation with my eyes open. Enjoy it for what it is not what I wish it was."

Rick knocked on the door, I made him wait a few mins, when I opened the door he looked me up and down, then drew a sharp breath. My mini skirt and tight white shirt made his body react so much I saw his bulge even through his pants. "Wow, you look great!" He stepped through the door and watched as I closed and locked it. "I haven't seen your hair down since I got back, it's beautiful."

"Thanks, you look great too."

We stood there for a second feeling awkward. We'd had sex a few days ago, but somehow that didn't make the personal connection part any easier. I was still in love with him and was trying my hardest to pretend it was just sex and I was okay with that. I think he could see right through my act. But I played the part anyway and for both our sanity he played along as well.

"Let's go into the living room, you put in a movie and I'll pour some wine."

"Sounds great." Putting the pizza on the coffee table and looking through the movies he had picked out Rick asked "Do you want to watch comedy or horror first?"

"Let's start with the scary one then the comedy. If I try to sleep after watching a scary movie, I'll be up all night hearing imaginary noises."

Rick put the movie in and sat back on the couch. I turned off the lights and settled back against the cushions. He handed me a glass of wine and lifted his for a toast. "Here's to rekindling old friendships."

Our glasses met as did our eyes. I noticed the delicate chime of the crystal and the deep pools of his eyes. After a moment of just staring at each other he broke the spell with a cough. "Okay, enough drama, bring on the horror flick!"

Rick laughed then pushed the play button on the remote. I could tell he didn't really notice the movie, he kept glancing at me. I think he wanted to touch me but he didn't want to scare me off. I guess he decided to go with the obviously corny; he faked a giant yawn and placed his arm around my shoulder. Laughing at his silly antic, but turned on by it nonetheless I leaned against him and snuggled against his chest. I felt something hard pressing against my hip, I reached down to see what it was. He stood up quickly and removed the pistol from his hip.

He saw the look on my face. "I'm sorry, it's habit, I always carry it." He removed it, cleared it and placed it on the coffee table.

As he was sitting down again, I think he noticed that I was staring at the pistol. He sat a little farther than he had been before. I reached for his hand and pulled him closer to me. "The gun doesn't bother me. Actually, that client that I told you about that was in my office a few days ago, I think he had that exact gun on his belt. M1911 right?" Leaning closer to the pistol without letting go of his hand, "it even had the same symbol on the grip. What does that mean?"

"That's the symbol for my unit. Only the men on my team were given this gun. I need to know everything about him." He stared at me for a moment, then started asking me questions about the client with the gun. I told him everything I could remember. After a few moments he shook his head and leaned back against the couch.

"Rick, do I need to worry? You seem worried?"

Taking a deep breath, Rick sighed. "There's nothing for you to worry about. I'll handle it. Did you get the address of the house he wanted you to renovate?"

I went to my bag and got out my notebook, I handed him the address. "You going to tell me what's going on?"

Rick grabbed his phone and texted the address to someone. Then he turned his phone off, reached for my waist and pulled me onto his lap. I straddled him and he started kissing me. It was then that I forgot about the movie, the gun, the creepy client and everything else. The warmth of his body brought back a flood of memories. Having already made the decision to let my body lead the way tonight, I wrapped my arms around Rick's waist and laid my head on his chest. Rick tightened his arm around me and we closed our eyes to enjoy holding each other. I looked up into his dark eyes. "Kiss me." I whispered.

Our lips joined slowly, almost as if we were afraid of breaking the spell by moving too fast. As the kiss deepened I could feel a fire rage in my heart, an all-consuming flame that had been smoldering within me all these years, and had always been ignored or covered with anger. Rick ran his hands down my back; my body once that of a girl, so thin and hard, now had the sexy shape of a grown woman. I knew I was curvy and soft in all the right places, he wanted to touch me, taste me. I wanted to let him. Letting his hands move to my hips he pulled me against his body. He knew I could feel his cock pressing against my thighs and core. I slid one hand down his chest and cupped him gently through his pants, I started slowly rubbing his hardness.

Rick broke the kiss and looked into my eyes. "If we keep this up I'm going to make love with you, we'll miss the movie."

I smiled at him and reached for the remote, turning off the TV I stood and took his hand. "Well, since I plan on keeping this up, we better move to a different room." Rick pulled me against his chest as he stood up, with me lifted in his arms and our lips joined in hungry passion he walked down the hall with me pointing to the correct door. He was surprised when he opened the door and realized it was the bathroom. He loosened his arms and let me slide down his body until my feet touched the floor. I walked into the room and lit the candles I had put out earlier. I pushed a button on a little remote and soft music filled the apartment.

"I believe you said something about a bath?" I reached up and started unbuttoning his shirt. As I revealed a section of his muscled chest I pressed my lips against his warm skin. I pushed the shirt off his shoulders and let it drop to the floor. Undoing his belt, I looked up into his eyes suddenly unsure I could do this again without paying a heavy price. Sensing my indecision. He took my head in his hands and kissed me. With our lips joined he stepped out of his shoes. He released my head and removed his pants, then slid his hands beneath my shirt and up my rib cage. He let his thumbs rub my nipples through the lacey bra I wore. I broke the kiss and pulled my own shirt off anxious now to be skin to skin. I had intentionally turned up the air conditioner and as I removed the bra I felt my nipples harden in the cool air. Next came the skirt which I threw against the wall with the rest. Smiling shyly at him I pulled my long hair into a loose knot on the back of my head then turned to the tub and started running the bath.

Rick leaned one sexy hip against the sink and watched as I bent as the waist and added oils and bubbles. I knew he could see my center, judging by his deepening breath I knew he was enjoying the view. A gentle aroma filled the room. I stood and turned toward him, he reached for my hand and pulled me against him. I went willingly into his arms, and let him kiss my face and neck. His hands held my waist and he slid his fingers into the elastic of my lacey panties. As his kiss returned to my lips he pulled apart the flimsy material and let the torn garment float to the floor. "If we keep this up I'm going to buy stock in panty companies!"

Laughing gently, I pushed his underwear down and felt his erect manhood spring forward as the confining material was moved. I stepped out of his arms and into the tub. He stared at the bubbles as they caressed my naked skin. "Are you getting in?"

As he let his body sink into the hot water his legs brushed against mine and I marveled at the feeling of our hot wet skin touching.

"Come here let me wash your back." I turned around and sat with my back to him; his legs surrounded me and guided my attention to the heat from his body where it met mine. His hands felt rough yet amazingly tender as he lathered my back. He poured the warm water down my back and watched as the bubbles slid down my smooth skin. I leaned back against his broad chest, his arms came around me and pulled us closer together. I smelled the soft scent of his soap, the way it felt to be held again made me realize how much I had missed him over the years. Just as he had done so many times before, he kissed the top of my shoulder then kissed up the side of my neck. I slid one hand behind the small of my back between our bodies to caress his cock. The skin was just as soft as the erection was hard. He slid his hands down my chest stopping to teasingly pinch my nipples, then his fingers circled the belly button ring he'd never noticed. My eyes were closed and my head dropped back against his shoulder as one hand expertly began rubbing my clit. His finger circled then pressed and rubbed until I was moaning out loud and squeezing his cock. His other hand moved even lower so he could slide two fingers in my wet pussy and move against my g-spot at the perfect pace and angle. I came in mere seconds. He stayed motionless until I released my grip on his rock-hard cock.

I turned in his arms to kiss him and the passion we shared surpassed anything I had felt before. Moving as smoothly as my shaking body would allow, I straddled his hips just as I had done on the couch. We both gasped as his cock slid into my pussy. We moved slowly at first, letting the warm water caress us as we rocked against each other. He seemed so in control while I called out his name and forgot how to breathe. As he got closer to the edge he gripped my hips and held me still as he set the pace he needed to cum. The faster he moved the harder his pubic bone hit against my clit. We came together. I could feel the heat of his orgasm as his cock exploded inside me.

Barely able to breathe I collapsed against his chest, where we stayed for several minutes listening to each other's hearts regain normal patterns. The water was getting cool. "Come on, let's go to the bedroom. We haven't had sex on the bed yet!"

Laughing we stepped out of the tub, I blew out the candles and took his hand. As I led him down the hall to my bedroom he watched the sexy sway of my hips. I knew he remembered holding my hips many years ago. There were lots of things I couldn't forget and figured he hadn't either, maybe watching my naked body brought back all those memories for him and caused his erection to come back so quickly. I didn't know they could do that. I walked into my room and sat on the bed and looked at Rick. He sat beside me and leaned in for a kiss. It was a few seconds after our lips met before I leaned against him and our arms went around one another. The blazing fire wasn't gone only replaced with a smoldering heat. This time would be slower, more tender. Or so I thought.

His mouth left mine and traveled down the side of my neck. He gently bit and kissed the spot where neck and shoulder meet that still drives me wild. Softly he pushed me back onto the bed. "My turn." He growled at me. Once again his lips moved, they left a trail of fire down my chest, stopping to wetly caress each nipple. He drew my breasts into his mouth and the heat from his tongue seemed to sear my skin, I could feel the pressure of his teeth on my nipple and he staked his claim on my body. Continuing his journey, he left my nipples and moved down toward my stomach. I moaned aloud when his tongue played with my belly button ring. Pausing only long enough to position himself between my knees, Rick's tongue found my wet pussy. As he kissed and licked my center I groaned in ecstasy and grabbed handfuls of blanket to try to control my body. His teeth found my clit and he gently nibbled the sensitive hub. The feeling of his hot wet tongue alternating with his teasing precise teeth and his fingers inside me caressing my G-spot made my body burn, I felt the fire starting and could do nothing to stop it even if I wanted to.

I couldn't fight the wave of sensation any longer and I cried out as I spiraled over the edge.

"Rick, please!"

He moved so his body covered mine. He paused and I opened my eyes. I could see the questions in his eyes behind the passion. "Are you sure this is what you want?" Not wanting to stop and think about the consequences, I took his face in my hands "Shut up and fuck me." I lifted up to capture his lips for a soul searing kiss. With our lips locked together Rick slowly joined our bodies. He slid his cock completely within me then paused. "No. This time we make love Becky." I started moving my hips trying to be one with him. He growled and grabbed my wrists, he put my arms over my head and held them there. "If you keep moving like that this will be over much too soon. I want it to last this time." He kissed my neck then started drawing little circles with his tongue. The tingles went from my neck straight to my clit. After a few seconds, he started moving within me. Together we created a rhythm as old as time yet as thrilling as the first time. Together we plunged over the edge of ecstasy. Rick released my arms and I ran my fingers in his hair pulling him closer to my lips. Our mouths joined and we became one being. Rick thrust into me fully and I felt my body stretch to accommodate his length, then his hot explosion deep within me.

We made love again and again, and fucked some more too. Yes, I know he knew the difference. It was almost as if we were memorizing each other's bodies. As we lay against one another, each shielding the other from the outside world, I found myself thinking of the future. If only...

Finally, I fell asleep in his arms.

CHAPTER 7

Rick

He lay in the bed watching her sleep. He wanted nothing more than to protect her from the world. His fingers ran softly down her cheek brushing a stray curl out of her face. She turned and snuggled her body against his, and he wished that he could just put his arm around her and go back to sleep. Cursing his career choice for the millionth time, he moved away from her and got up as quietly as possible. Moving silently into the living room he retrieved his phone. It took it a moment to power on but the message that awaited him made him want to scream.

"Affirmative, the guy at the farm house is Burt. Are we moving or not?"

He wasn't concerned with the fact that it had been hours sent the text came in. Stevens and Stevens would not move without word from him. Really pissed him off that he was having to go take care of this, it should have been over months ago. Not wanting her to think he had deserted her he looked for pen and paper and left her a note telling her he would call her tonight. He only hoped he could.

Getting dressed and folding her clothes in the chair, he sat the note where she would see it and left the apartment. Once in his car headed down the street he called Stevens. The phone only rang once before he answered. "What's up Ghost? We handling this tonight or what?"

"Why so anxious Dagger, got somewhere you'd rather be?"

"As a matter of fact, got me a fine woman asleep on my bed and I'd love to put the availability to good use."

Rick laughed, "Damn bad guys, always getting in the way. Meet up at the God's house 20 minutes." The conversation ended. He dialed another number and had a surprisingly similar conversation with Bear. He felt a moments sympathy for his team, he completely understood not wanting to walk away from a naked woman tonight. Eighteen minutes later he pulled up to the small one story Tudor on the south side of Nashville. The porch light was off, telling him to go to the garage doors on the side of the house. The gate was open so he turned off his lights and drove the car around back where it would be shielded by woods. Stevens, and Bear were already there. He entered the basement, patted the dogs and smiled at the obscene pile of weapons on the table. "You guys think we have enough gear?"

"I think we need to be a little more cautious here. If we take him tonight we won't know why he's here."

"I hear you but this is my call and I want this done with. If we can take him tonight we'll get the info we want then drop his ass off a cliff. If we can't take him I want that building bugged from top to bottom."

"Yes sir." Rick didn't pull rank often but he was tired and ready to move on with his life. The men looked at each other for a second then started changing into solid black, and strapping on weapons like they were preparing for war. Hopefully this wouldn't be a long night. They had a job to do tomorrow morning, an assassination to stop actually and they needed the sleep.

The drive out to the farm house was completed in silence. Each man was preparing for a fight that they prayed wouldn't come. The house came into view and the vehicle stopped. Not saying a word each man pulled his mask down to cover his face and drew his fire arm of choice, as a unit they started working their way toward the seemingly empty building.

Becca

The next morning, I woke alone. Assuming Rick was in the shower I padded across the room and took my robe off the back of the door. It was then that I realized the clothes we had discarded the night before were in the chair and Rick's clothes were gone. He wasn't in the bathroom, with a growing sense of dread I walked into the kitchen. There was a note on the counter.

> Good morning Beautiful,
> Sorry I had to leave so early. You looked so peaceful I didn't want to wake you. Last night meant more to me than you'll ever understand. I'll call you tonight.
> Forever and a day,
> Rick

I leaned against the counter in shock. "He left! He just left." Looking at my amazed

reflection in the glass of the microwave door I stood up and asked myself, "What did you expect? Declarations of love? You knew this was how it would be, get over it!" I squared my shoulders and nodded. "Okay, back to being alone." As

I stomped back down the hall I muttered out loud, "I really need to stop talking to myself!"

The rest of the day went pretty much just like every other Sunday. I had breakfast, did some yoga, cleaned the house, did some paperwork, then met my parents for dinner. They could tell something was wrong but they didn't ask and I didn't share.

After dinner I cuddled on the couch with Tori in my arms and watched a little TV. After tucking her in I headed for my room. Just as I was opening a Cosmo the phone rang. "Hello?"

"Hey girl! How was the big date?"

My heart felt very heavy suddenly. "Hi Christy, it was fine."

"Okay, put down the book and tell me the truth."

I took a deep breath, "the night was perfect, but he was gone when I woke up this morning. He was supposed to call today but he hasn't."

"Oh Beck! I'm so sorry. Are you okay? Want me to come over? I have booze!"

"I'm fine, I was just using him to relieve a little stress, no big deal. No need to come over, I'm going to bed now anyway. We'll talk tomorrow."

I hung up the phone, turned off the lamp, and cried myself to sleep.

CHAPTER 8

Monday seemed to drag by. I did all the things I normally do on a Monday. Talk to clients, the Thompson's had learned they were having a baby and needed to change a few things in their design plan to accommodate the new addition. Set up the schedule for the week and made my shopping list for fabric and things. At 1 o'clock Christy got back from lunch and I headed out. "After I grab a bite to eat I'm going to hit the fabric store; we need quite a bit of that burgundy tapestry material." I had lunch at Toot's (there is just something about chicken wings and curly fries!). It was a pretty normal lunch, just me and my laptop, but I kept getting that feeling like I was being watched. Then I stopped at Hancock's for the material. Again, I felt like someone was way too interested in my day to day activities. Linda, the manager, was sitting behind the counter watching the news. As she was ringing up my items I caught the end of the story she was watching. 'No one was hurt in the drive by today at the downtown office building. In what was apparently an attempted mob hit several shots were fired at the entrance to the Morgan building. The surprise here is the return fire that came from several of the second story windows across the street blowing the rear tires on the car and forcing the mobsters to stop and exit their vehicle. The police were then able to capture the two men who have now claimed to have diplomatic immunity. No further details have been released at this time and no country of origin has been given for the two gunmen. The metro police chief acknowledged that without the help of the unknown shooters from the second story the gunmen would have escaped however they want to insist that civilians allow the police to do their jobs and not interfere.'

I almost convinced myself not to think about that story, not to read too much into it. There is no way it could have anything to do with Rick. He was retired. But the seed was planted. Diplomatic Immunity? That means they are part of some foreign government. Wait, the news had said it was the Morgan building. Rick had business downtown this morning and he had said something about meeting an old friend for lunch in the restaurant in the bottom of the Morgan building!

As if I wasn't doing a good enough job freaking myself out, I saw the creepy client from the office sitting in the parking lot. He was in his car reading the paper. He never looked up at me, but I knew it was him. Something told me not to let him know I recognized him. I kept walking and got to my car in what I hoped was a casual fashion.

I managed to keep my ranting (and my freak out) to myself until I walked into my office. I slammed the door and started screaming "Oh hell no! I am not being a part of this anymore! He lied to me again. I am so done!!!" Christy stuck her head around the corner and looked at me.

"Everything ok?"

I considered not telling her about my outing but needed to tell someone. Remaining calm became more and more difficult as I went on. But I finally got all the info out.

Christy looked terrified, "That guy was in here today! He wanted your cell phone number, something about needing you to come view his farm house sooner than he thought. I told him you had a meeting and had left your phone here."

The bottom fell out of my stomach. I really needed to talk to Rick. What the hell was going on here. "Was probably a coincidence, I have a lot of work to do, why don't you head on out?" I know she could see the fear in my eyes but she didn't push it.

I forced myself to concentrate on work until Christy left, then I picked up Tori and headed back home. I was exhausted. Both mentally and physically. I double checked all the locks on the doors and windows before I headed upstairs.

I had dinner, played with Tori awhile and put her to bed, then I decided to soak in a hot bath and try to forget my stupidity. After a few minutes I got a text from Christy, she was down stairs and was coming in, she didn't want to sneak up on me. She knocked on the bathroom door and walked in. "Hey, I'm taking the little woman with me tonight." Sitting on the closed lid of the toilet she picked up the towel and placed it on her lap. "Any word from whats-his-name?"

I didn't bother to open my eyes, mainly because I knew Christy would notice they were bloodshot from crying and that conversation wasn't one I was ready for just yet. "His name is Rick and no he hasn't called. Probably won't either. I'm willing to bet he's off on some mission to save the world again."

"Yeah probably. Anyway, I'm leaving now. See

ya!" Christy had left the door to the bathroom open so I heard her leave and the lock engage. In serious need of a glass of wine (or maybe a bottle) I sat up and opened the drain. My towel wasn't on the sink where I'd left it. Thinking I had maybe left it on the bed I let the water drip off my body as I brushed my teeth and washed my face. As I was walking down the hall to the bedroom I heard a noise in the kitchen. I ran to the bedroom and grabbed my robe and the gun I kept under the edge of my mattress. Then I tip toed back toward the kitchen. With the gun down by my thigh just as I had been taught in class. I peeked around the corner of the door and saw Rick looking thru my kitchen drawers.

"What the hell are you doing?"

Guess I startled him because he yanked on the drawer he had been in and it fell to the floor. "Holy shit! You were supposed to be in the tub."

"I was, then I got out of MY tub in MY house to

find a stranger in MY kitchen going thru MY drawers. How did you get in here anyway?"

He looked at me with a strange look on his face. "Stranger? Really?"

I tried to look apologetic for calling him a stranger but really, after today it was obvious I didn't know him anymore. "Sorry, you know what I mean though. It was an extremely stressful day. Let me guess, Christy let you in?"

"Yes, she came up the sidewalk while I was standing outside trying to decide if I should call or just knock." He had the common sense to look embarrassed at least. He eyed my handgun with a little bit of unease. "I was looking for a bottle opener for the wine. Want some?"

I sighed, getting over him was going to be impossible if he kept coming back looking so sexy! "Yes, please. The opener is in the drawer you dropped. I'll go put my gun away and put on some pajamas. You can wait in the living room." Back in my room, the gun and magazine separated and put in the correct places I pulled the pjs that matched the robe from the dresser and let it slide down my body. As the silk brushed my nipples I remembered the feel of his tongue in that same place and almost forgot to be mad at him for leaving and not calling and for what I suspected (using me as just a piece of ass while he was in town on another stupid mission.).

Almost.

Mostly comfortable in my pjs and robe I went back into the living room expecting to hear him talk about leaving or taking it slow or some other excuse to be walking out of my life again. I tried to walk past him to sit on the other end of the couch. He reached up and grabbed my waist to pull me down into his lap. My arms instinctively went around h]is neck to balance myself. "Rick, please, we can't do this anymore."

"Why can't we? Don't you feel the sparks between us?"

"Yes, I feel them, I felt them and missed them every day for the past four years. Alone. But in a few days or weeks or whenever you catch those men from the shooting today, you'll go back to your life and forget about me all over again. I don't want to hurt that way again. I don't have that many tears left." I tried to get up but his arms were like steel bands around me. "and I can't put Tori in that kind of danger either."

"I'm sorry I hurt you, I didn't realize you felt that way. But I'm not going anywhere. I've accepted a consulting position here. I'll be home every night. I'd like the home I come to, to be ours. Yours and mine."

I stopped trying to get up and just stared at him. "What? You said you could never work in an office, that's one of the reasons you started those stupid missions in the first place. Before we can talk about anything else I need you to be honest with me. The gun fire downtown, how are you involved? I thought you were retired."

He took a deep breath, "I am retired. There is a man here, looking for me and my team. He wants revenge for us killing his family during our escape. We know where he lives and we've wired his place. It won't be long before we capture him and then it will all be over."

"The gun fight downtown?"

"The consulting job I took is actually the beginning of my own security agency. The fight was staged, blanks, no real danger. It was designed to show Mr. Morgan that we can protect him without any trouble or collateral damage, and without anyone knowing we exist."

I looked at my hands in my lap, unsure I wanted the answers to my next question. "Tell me about while you were gone. The mission, your capture, the scars, how you escaped. Everything."

"You don't want to those images in your head."

"I want to know, I want to hate those men as much as you do.

Rick

He thought for a moment about lying to her again. But decided to try the truth this time. He released her waist to allow her to get up, he was relieved when she sat still and listened. "I'll tell you the basics, but I'm not going to be responsible for you having nightmares for the rest of your life. My last mission was to go undercover and become part of terrorist ring out of Afghanistan. I had no way to know how long I would be gone or if I would even ever return home. I managed to not only join the cell but become a pretty high ranking member of the leader's personal security detail. I kept complete informational notes and we managed to track the cell's hierarchy all the way to the crowned prince. We saw the atrocities the men of that group put the people of the village through, so after I sent my transmission to our people, the prince somehow discovered the information and had us arrested and imprisoned. Someone on our side had sold us out. All of our belongings were confiscated. Our bags were thrown in a corner and forgotten. For almost three years we were used as slaves for the cell, they either worked the hell out of us or tortured us. That's where the scars come from. The old man in charge died suddenly and his grandson came in to take over, he eventually had someone go through our bags that had been sitting in a pile collecting dust. At first I thought it didn't matter because surely our gadgets had all died. I didn't expect one of their men to have a charger that would fit my laptop. They charged it up and started going through all my files." Here he paused and looked directly into her eyes. "On my laptop. There had been a lot of info on that computer. I had wiped the hard drive daily with the software I was provided. But I still had no way of knowing what they knew about my men, their families, myself or people I cared about not to mention the info I had been feeding our government. They had all 3 of us in a cell where they could see us as they went thru our things. We were only able to talk at night, but we managed to work out an escape plan. The afternoon before we broke out they started going thru the computer. They were really pissed at how little info there was but the guard said he thought it would be enough to work. We had no way of knowing what they were planning but we had to let someone know. Someone we could trust. We escaped that night and took the laptop and all our papers, I killed the two men who had gone through our stuff. We got to Egypt and flew home. There was lots of time to talk on the plane. We got our stories straight and decided to join the civilian world and leave the danger behind, we had all had enough." He paused to collect his thoughts and carefully choose his phrasing for what was left to tell. Her hands took his and held on tight. "We followed our plans, gave the reports to the correct people then resigned with the agreement amongst each other to never speak of it again. About a month ago, I got a call from Dave, one of the men; James, and his wife and young son were killed in a car accident. At first we didn't think anything about it, tragic but not a hit or anything. Then we got the details, all three of them had been shot, execution style then placed in the car and it was set on fire. It had been a hit." Rick felt her body tighten and he prepared to let her go without a fight. "Dave and his girlfriend are in hiding right now. Someone was following her and tried to get into her building. If it wasn't for the old super who doesn't open the door to people he doesn't know, she would be dead."

This time she did get up. "Why are you really here Rick, and don't tell me you missed me."

Rick stood up, he couldn't sit there with as much nervous energy as he had. "When Dave told me about his girlfriend I figured they had found about her from something on the laptop. But Dave told me he didn't even meet her until after he retired. I had to be close to you, to protect you just in case they somehow found out you are important to me. I called Jon and Nita, they told me you had moved to the city and started this business. When I found your website I saw one of the pictures had Victoria in it. I just couldn't stand by and not protect the woman I love and her child. I didn't come here to disrupt your life; I came to protect it. I don't know if you are in any danger baby, but just in case you are I needed to be here. I never intended to let you know I was here. But I couldn't be this close and not touch you. I love you Becca."

Becca

He looked at me like I should just swoon and fall into his arms or something! I may have too, if it hadn't been for the danger he brought with him. I started pacing, my body as wired as my mind. "You came here with the intention of protecting my family? What, am I supposed to feel safer now? How dare you? Any danger in my life is because of you. You know what; if you had done the right thing all those years ago you wouldn't have left. Do you have any idea how long it took to get my life back on track after you left? Two years! I waited for two years for you to call or write or something. While you were off in the desert somewhere I was going thru hell, I went thru the whole pregnancy and then buried our daughter all alone! Do you have any idea what that felt like? It was the hardest thing I've ever had to do and I had to do it without you! Now you expect me to feel all better because you missed me and because you suffered too. I'm telling you right now, if anything at all happens to my daughter you won't have to worry about protecting anyone except yourself."

I stormed out of the room toward my bedroom. Rick followed me. He caught up with me just inside my room; "What pregnancy? What daughter? I knew nothing about any of that! How can you be mad at me for not being here for something I didn't know was going on?" I jerked my arm out of his grasp and sat on the bed. I let the story spill out and managed, barely, to keep the tears from doing the same. When I stopped talking he looked like I'd hit him. But I didn't feel sorry for him at all. He brought killers to my daughter's life, screw him.

"I'm sorry Becca, and I'm sorry I wasn't here for the pain you went thru, but I will keep you and Tori safe and when this is all over I'll get you to understand and forgive me. Because I plan to be here for the next one."

"The next one? What the hell makes you think I want to have a child with you? I have Tori and she is all the family I need. I got on with my life eventually after you left last time and I will get on with it this time too. Just get out and leave us alone. Take care of your business from a distance. As long as you are not a part of our lives they'll know we mean nothing to you and they will leave us alone." I turned away from him and tried to slam the door in his face. He reached out and pulled me into his arms and held me tight. I struggled but his arms were bands of steel. "Becca, listen to me. I came back because I love you. I never should have left the way I did I know that now. And maybe I've let things go too far too fast this time. Had I known there would be anything dangerous for you because of me I would have stayed away. But now that I'm here I have to keep you safe. I can do that from a distance but my heart won't let me stay away from you, and I can't be around you and not touch you." He held me tight and told me over and over how he loved me. I tried not to listen to him, I really did. But the more I tried to get away the more

I realized I wanted to be in his arms right now; even if I couldn't stay there. I stopped fighting him, and myself. "Rick, you broke my heart once, please don't do it again." Laying my head against his chest I inhaled the scent of him and waited for him to make the next move. He put his finger under my chin and lifted my face to his.

"I'll never hurt you again. I promise."

I felt his lips on my hair and when I tilted my head back to gaze up at him, he trailed kisses down my face until he found my mouth. This kiss was not a gentle brush of his lips against mine as our first kiss had been, nor was it a kiss of all consuming passion like the last one we shared. No, this was a real kiss. A deep passionate, heart-pounding, soul-mending, major league kiss, and without hesitation I opened my lips (and my heart) to him.

I started to undo his shirt, I kissed his chest then pushed the shirt off of his arms. I removed my robe and let it fall to the floor at his feet. Sitting on the edge of the bed I undid his belt and opened his pants. Pushing them from his hips I let my hands run up the back of his thighs. I removed his briefs and smiled up at the shocked look on his face. I started at his belly button and ran my lips and tongue down his hard cock. His body was rigid and I could feel him throbbing in my mouth as I pulled him closer to me. He tangled his hands in my hair and moved with my rhythm as I pleasured him. I cupped my fingers under his balls and could feel them drawing up as he grabbed my hair and started pulsing his hot cum down my throat. His hands gripped the back of my head and pulled me away from his penis. I could see his still hard cock wet from my mouth as he dropped to his knees in front of the bed he grinned at me. "It's my turn." He kissed my neck and slowly pushed me back against the bed. His lips left a trail of fire over my breasts and down my belly. My body trembled as his mouth found my sensitive swollen clit. His lips and tongue drove me wild, his two fingers inside my pussy on my g-spot started a fire. I begged him to stop but only half meant it. I felt the heat build until I thought I was going to explode. Plunging over the edge I filled his mouth with my cum. He slowed then moved away from my pussy. Unable to speak I patted the spot next to me in invitation. We'd had sex many times before thru the years, but this was different. We lay there for a long time just kissing, touching and memorizing each other's bodies. I knew we would have some serious decisions to make in the morning. When we could stand it no longer he cradled me against his body. Joining out lips first, he entered me in a smooth motion that left us both breathless. We made love slowly, enjoying each other's bodies and letting our touches say things our pride wouldn't let us say out loud. The taste of my own juices on his lips and tongue combined with the hot pumping cock between my legs and forced an orgasm from me that was more intense than any I've ever felt before. It was as if my heart swelled with love at the same time that he thrust deep within me and exploded, filling me with his liquid heat.

Later as we lay in each other's arms, I was on the verge of sleep with my head of his chest. "Are you asleep?"

I felt his voice rumble in his chest. "Not yet." All I could muster was a sleepy murmur.

"I was just wondering something."

"What's that?" I hoped it was nothing to dramatic, I wanted this moment to last forever.

"Should we get married in a church or at the park?"

Suddenly very much awake I forced myself to stay still. "Married?"

"Yes, I love you, you love me. Tori needs a father, and we haven't exactly been using birth control this week so you may be pregnant again. This time I will be here for the whole thing. No matter what. Since we are going to be having children we should at least get married." He sat up, causing me to sit up as well. "If you'll have me that is."

"When I found out I was pregnant I decided to keep

the baby because she would be a part of you, and at least I would have that. I was really happy the whole time. I started a million letters of my own, I wanted to tell you but didn't know what to say. When they told me she was gone I died too." He pulled me into his arms but didn't say anything. I think he could tell I wasn't done talking. "When I buried her I tried to tell myself that I was burying my feelings for you as well. I tried to move on, really, I did. But every guy I went out with just didn't measure up. The chance to adopt Tori came and I couldn't pass it up. She filled the hole left by Lily's death. Are you sure you want to take on a baby that isn't yours?"

He took a deep breath, his chest rising and falling as if he were taking in my words. "At first I was mad that you didn't tell me about Lily. But it only took me a few seconds before I realized that if you had felt you could tell me you would have. We were children back then. If we had gotten married, we would probably have been driven apart by the sorrow of her death. I wasn't ready to be a father then, I am now. I want to be your husband and Tori's father, and I want to have lots more kids with you." I was so still in his arms I guess he thought I had fallen asleep. "What are you thinking about?"

I sat up and straddled his lap so I could look directly into his eyes. "If we get married I need your word that there will be no secrets, no lies, no half-truths. I want and deserve total honesty and loyalty."

He looked at me for a moment then nodded. "You have my word."

"I was also thinking how pretty the park will be in September and that I could plan a perfect wedding in six months."

He looked surprised for a split second and then he rolled us over and we were kissing and laughing.

As happy as I was I just couldn't shake the feeling something bad was coming. "Rick, I want to meet your friends. You say this team of yours was with you over there and you guys are working together here, you said you would keep us safe. I need to know them, I need them to know me and Tori."

"No problem. But why do you need them to know you guys?"

"I want them to protect us because they want to, not just because you tell them too."

"Baby, you and Tori are part of me, that makes you family. My family, their family. They would die to protect you just like I would die to protect someone that is family to them. But yes I want you to meet them. Maybe we can do a BBQ?"

"Sounds perfect."

Rick

Feeling Becca's body against his made him hard, hearing her say she would marry him made him the happiest man alive, knowing he had to find Burt Sedoris and kill him as fast as possible scared him to death. Knowing the bad guy was out there had never scared him before, but then he had never had so much to lose.

The next morning they woke up late and had no time for making love like he wanted. They did make excellent use of the shower though. He used his laptop and checked the cameras around the building. No signs of Burt. After a way to short kiss, he left Becca in her office and headed out of town.

Pulling his black jeep into the private garage he changed clothes, the black on black look was starting to get on his nerves but for today it served his purpose, and if all went well it would be the last time he wound need them.

He placed a call, loaded the back of the jeep and

started looking at the maps. Just as he started to formulate the plan a 'sensible' gray Nissan pulled into the garage. Stevens stepped out of the car dressed in all black as well. The 2 men laughed at the old joke that they looked like robbers. They shook hands.

"Got some news last night. Sammy's pregnant." Stevens paused. "Rick I need today to be the day we move on." Stevens didn't have to say much more than that. Rick put his hand on his friends shoulder, the closest they would get to a hug.

"I'm ready too brother, we all need to be able to start fresh. He made contact with Becca last week. I had to wait til she was out of the office before I could get the client file she had made on him. The bastard pretended to be a client with a farmhouse for her to fix. Turns out the farmhouse is real enough, the boys and I rigged it a few days ago. He hadn't been there in a few days, but the sensor picked up a lot of movement this morning. That's where we are headed first. I hope we catch him there but if not that will give us an idea where to look next."

"We sure it's just him?"

"I haven't seen anything to say otherwise. He was the only one who knew what we were doing and had access to the prince to rat us out." Rick looked at the pile of weapons in the back of the jeep. "Think that's enough?"

Stevens looked the pile over, drew his hunting knife out of the side of his boot and grinned. "The guns are yours sissy boy, I've got my weapon of choice right here."

The men clapped each other on the back and got into the jeep. The farmhouse wasn't far but they rode in silence. Each thinking of the person they were protecting.

About 15 mins later Rick pulled the jeep into the woods beside the road and parked it. He went back to cover the tracks showing their location and Stevens stepped out and started strapping on weapons. At Rick's look he grinned. "Just because I prefer the blade doesn't mean I don't want a gun handy. I'm picky not stupid." They walked the last mile to the farmhouse. The black Lincoln he had seen on the video at Becca's was parked in the driveway, with the trunk door open and a white tennis shoe on the ground behind the car.

Rick felt his heart drop, Burt had Becca. How the hell had he gotten her and beaten them here? He started to bolt for the house. Stevens laid a hand on his shoulder. "Slow and safe dude. We can't help her if he hears us coming." Rick took a deep breath and stuck to the plan. They headed around the perimeter to the side of the house with no windows. From the visit the other night, he knew there were no cameras. Using the cover of the existing landscape they reached the wall and went in opposite directions around the house. Rick reached the back door about the same time Stevens reached the front door. They could see each other through the empty house. Opening the doors at the same time they entered silently.

The layout consisted of one big room in the middle with a kitchen on one end, bedroom and bathroom on the other. They looked at each other to decide their next move when they heard the scream come from the bedroom.

Both men turned and headed for the bedroom door. Stevens reached it first and kicked it in, he went in and left and Rick went in and right. Burt was standing beside the bed with his belt in his hand and his pants sliding down his legs. The woman on the bed was naked, with a bag over her head and her hands tied to the headboard. Rick felt rage fly through him at the knowledge of what this bastard was planning to do to her. He shot him in the knee. Burt went down cussing.

"You're a dead man Dorsey!! You're all dead! First I'm going to kill you two, then I'm going to torture and kill every person you love, including that cute little woman and child of yours." Just as Rick lifted his gun to take the kill shot, Burt rolled toward the bed and reached under it.

Before he could grab his hidden gun Stevens drew his arm back and threw his knife. It buried itself in Burt's heart.

It took about 4 seconds for Burt's body to register that it was dying, then 1 more second for him to draw his last breath. Rick grabbed the bastard away from the bed and threw his body up against the wall. Stevens covered the woman with a blanket and removed the bag from her head. Rick saw her face and released the breath he didn't even realize he'd been holding. It was not Becca. "Sammy!! Oh God, I thought you were with your mom today. What did that bastard do to you?"

Sammy sat up on the bed and placed both hands on her still flat stomach. "He hadn't done anything yet." Her voice was shaky as she stood and leaned against Stevens.

Stevens pulled her to him. There were tears in his eyes that he didn't even attempt to hide. "Baby, he's dead, he can't hurt you or anyone else."

As Rick watched the couple cling to each other he

was overcome with the need to hold Becca.

"Let's head out Stevens. I want to get home to Becca and Tori."

The woman pulled the sheet around herself, stood, walked over to wear Burt's body lay against the wall. "His name was Burt?" She was staring at the body, emotionless.

Stevens placed his arm around her shoulder. "Yes."

"He was the bad guy." The lack of emotion on her face worried Rick. She walked over to the body, knelt down, closed Burt's eyes then stood and looked down at him. "Asshole." Then she turned and looked at Stevens. "I'm heading to the bath room, can you bring me my clothes." As she walked past Rick she smiled. "I always have to pee!"

The men looked at each other. "That's my woman. I can't wait to make her my wife. Guess I can do that now. I didn't want to propose while dick head was still around. Now my child will be born with a father. Thanks man."

Rick looked at the floor to let the uncomfortable moment

pass. "No problem dude." He wanted to get home and tell

Becca the danger was gone, she was safe.

CHAPTER 9

The next day I told Christy all about what had
happened between Rick and I. She was pretty skeptical at
first but she knew how much I loved him and how long I
had been in love with him. "Okay, wedding in the park in
six months? Have you called the park yet? I think you have
to reserve those pavilions ahead of time." She rambled on
about details for a few minutes then stopped. "What about
your mom and dad? What are they going to say about all
this? Don't they hate Rick?"

"They don't HATE him exactly. They are just upset
with him over what happened. Once they see how things
are turning out they'll come around." I hope!! Knowing I
would have to tell them eventually I decided to take the
bull by the horns so to speak and invite them over for
dinner this week. Picking up the phone to call my mom I
could see my hand shaking. On the fourth ring I was

breathing a sigh of relief and about to hang up, then my dad answered. "Hello daughter, how are you?" We talked small talk for a few minutes. "Okay, I can tell you have something you want to talk about so spill it already."

I took a deep breath and jumped right in… "I want you and mom to come to dinner on Thursday night. I have someone I want you to get to know."

"A man? You didn't even tell us you were dating! How long has he been around? Does he treat you well? How serious is it?" Typical dad! A dozen questions.

"Dad! Hold on, we've only been dating for a couple of weeks, but he's been around for years. We treat each other great. And… well, it's very serious. We are getting married in September." I stopped and waited for the next round of questions.

"Rick Dorsey?" That one question and the tone in his voice said it was going to be a very long dinner conversation on Thursday.

"Yes Dad. Rick. We've spent the last while together and we've done a lot of talking and crying and fixing things. There is a lot to the story that you don't know, that you can't know, but I know everything and I know it won't be easy and it won't be perfect. But I love him and he loves me. I've forgiven him for leaving, and he didn't know about any of the rest of it. Daddy, please try to be a little happy for me."

The silence from the other end was deafening, I heard his sigh then "Baby, I am happy for you. I just don't trust him. Your mother and I love you more than anything or anyone else on the planet. It's our job to worry about you. If you have decided to marry him then we will accept him and will do our best to like him. Just know that if he hurts you again I will hunt him down and kill him. Let me tell your mom, she will be in a bit of a shock over this. Are you okay? Really?"

"Thanks Daddy, it really is going to be okay. And I

am excellent! For the first time in a long time I really am."
We talked for a few more minutes about dinner on
Thursday, the said our goodbyes. That was easier than I
thought it would be. Now just to let Rick know he was
going to meet my parents again.

Thursday was pretty uneventful. Rick came over
early to help me get the food ready. He looked so damn
good in his khaki slacks and light blue polo shirt, (he
seemed to stay away from black lately) especially with a
sleeping Tori in his arms. He leaned against the counter and
made chit chat to try to help me not be so nervous. As soon
as the chicken was done and on the table he followed me
back into the kitchen. His arm came around my waist and I
turned in his embrace so I could see his face. "It will be
fine. We are all adults here." He kissed me and I seemed to
forget all about my parents and dinner and everything
except the feel of his lips against mine and how
comfortable he looked holding my daughter.

Until the knock on the door that is.

"See, you were very relaxed for a moment there." He patted my ass as I walked to the front door.

"Hi Mom, Daddy. Come on in. You remember Rick don't you?" At first they all just stood there looking at each other. My mom spoke first.

"Hello Rick. Welcome home. I trust you are here to stay this time?" She didn't wait for an answer she just reached out for Tori then headed for the kitchen where she was the most comfortable.

Dad looked at Rick and then held out his hand. "Just so you know son, if you break her heart again I'll hunt you down and kill you." They shook hands and that seemed to break the ice. Dinner took forever but at least it was civil. Dad didn't say much, and Mom jumped right in with the wedding planning. Rick sat beside me at the table, his knee against mine for support. Finally, it was over!

"Becky, I'll be here around 9, we can have

breakfast and make our 'to-do' lists. Rick you can come back and join us for breakfast before you go about your day. This is your wedding too and you need to stay in touch with what we are doing in case you have any ideas." Mom always loves having a project to plan and people to boss around. They took forever getting out the door, but finally I closed the door and locked it up. Rick was waiting at the top of the stairs for me. "What's this about coming back for breakfast?"

"Well maybe you should just spend the night. If you want to have more kids, we better start practicing."

Rick laughed as he swept me into his arms. "Sounds like a great plan to me." I giggled as he teased my neck with his tongue. "Wait, grab that bag off the top of the fridge, there's a few things I want to do." He sat me down on the kitchen counter, stood between my knees and kissed me deeply. He ran his hands up my thighs catching my skirt and pushing it out of the way. When his hands reached the heat of my pussy without any barriers his eyes widened then darkened with passion.

"No panties?"

"You keep ripping them to shreds and besides I wanted to entice you to stay tonight." I opened his pants just enough to free his cock, hard and straining against his briefs as evidence of his passion.

"Just try and get rid of me baby." He held his cock in one hand and rubbed its tip against my hot, wet pussy lips. The erotic teasing drove me mad.

"Make love to me, now."

Grabbing my hips, he thrust deep within me, "with you baby, never to you." Our bodies set the rhythm and our breathing quickened, heat and ecstasy exploded within us. As we kissed, I felt him growing within me again. I locked my legs around him and smiled. "Take me to bed."

Rick held me to him so our bodies stayed joined. Just the friction from walking down the hall with him inside me drew a groan from my throat. Pushing the door open to my room he lay me down on the bed and removed the rest of his clothes. He slid my skirt off and unbuttoned my blouse. The white lace of my bra was soft as his rough fingers traced the edge against my breasts. Sliding his fingers against the front clasps he removed my bra and freed my breasts to his exploring hands. His lips and tongue left a trail of fire everywhere he kissed. I pushed him back. "My turn to play." I reached into the bag from the kitchen, pulled out chocolate syrup and whipped cream. "I need a banana split." I drizzled syrup in a thin line down his tight stomach across his solid cock. He moaned as the warm syrup spread over his skin. I sprayed the cold whipped cream into my mouth then took him in between my lips, the sensation of the cold cream and the heat of my mouth made his hips lift off the bed. I moved my tongue across the sensitive skin just under the head of his cock and allowed him to set the rhythm as his cock inched in and out of my mouth. I felt his balls tighten in my hand just as he pulled me up against his body. "That's not how I'm going to cum tonight." His lips claimed mine as his hands found my nipples, he pinched and twisted them gently between his fingers as his tongue ravaged my mouth. When he had me moaning and ready to explode he stopped. "I want to try that. Lay down." I laid down on my back and let Rick pour the chocolate syrup over my body, his tongue roamed over my skin. I moaned again.

"Rick, I need to get the rest of the chocolate off of you."

He turned so we were facing opposite ends of the bed and put his knees on either side of my head. "Get me nice and clean baby." Then he leaned forward with his body completely draped over mine his mouth found my clit. He sucked on my magic button gently at first then his teeth nipped and I almost came. He slid his finger inside me and rubbed my G-spot. I felt the pressure building and didn't want to cum alone. Lifting my head I took the entire length of his cock in my mouth. As it passed over my tongue and down my throat he moved faster, driving us both to the edge. We enjoyed each other's mouths and tongues until we could stand it no longer. Rick rolled quickly off me and pulled me up against him. I straddled his hips and he thrust his cock inside me. We immediately found a rhythm and it was only seconds before we both exploded. I felt his heat spread through me. Neither of us moved and it was a moment before I realized he was still rock hard. I smiled at him and slowly started moving against him. We made love slowly this time, taking our time and exploring each other fully. Afterward, as we lay in each other's arms I started giggling. "What's so funny?"

"Look at these sheets! This chocolate will never come out."

Rick laughed, "We'll have to invest in rubber sheets! You throw these away, I'll warm up the shower."

The next two weeks flew by, Rick stayed at my place most nights. Starting his business was taking a lot of attention. I was planning a wedding, being pushed by Mom to spend every spare moment on the details. Finally, the only thing left to plan was the rehearsal dinner and my dress.

CHAPTER 10

"What do you mean you aren't wearing white?" Mom was pretending to be shocked. Christy was pretending not to laugh, and I was ignoring them both. The tea length champagne dress was perfect. I turned in front of the mirror and smiled as I imagined Rick taking this dress off of me on our first night as newlyweds.

"Never mind, your mind is obviously made up." Mom must have seen the look in my eyes. "Its beautiful baby, he won't be able to take his eyes off you." With the dress paid for I told Mom and Christy good evening and headed home. It had been a very long couple of weeks. I felt more tired than usual. I wanted a little alone time with Tori. The BBQ with all of Rick's friends was tomorrow and I needed some real sleep.

I took a quick shower and put on a t-shirt that Rick had left the last time he stayed the weekend. Tori fell asleep in my arms and I placed her in the cradle beside the couch and turned off the TV. My book wasn't on the end table, I got up and leaned over the arm to see if it was on the floor. "That's a very welcoming view." I practically fell off the couch.

"Rick, you scared the hell out of me. How did you get in? I didn't hear you knock."

He went from looking horny to intense in 2 seconds flat. "The door was unlocked downstairs and this one was standing open. Are you sure you locked them both?" He started looking at the lampshades and behind the picture frames.

"Yes, I locked them. I always do. Why were they opened? Was someone in here? You said that guy was dead. Maybe he wasn't working alone."

"Maybe you just thought they were locked, you've been really stressed out with planning the wedding and taking care of Tori. Just relax. They are locked now and we'll put new locks on everything in the morning. We went through all his papers, he was here alone." His little speech didn't really make either of us feel better but we sort of decided to ignore the nerves for the night. He did make a quick call. "Check the cameras at Becca's place. Let me know if you see anything out of the ordinary." He hung up the phone and leaned in for a quick kiss. "Benefits of having a security business."

"Okay, creeps officially gone. Now what were you saying about the view?" I turned my back to him and bent at the waist to pick up my book from the floor. He was staring at my ass. Sliding his hands around my hips he stepped in behind me, I felt his denim covered erection press against my naked backside.

"I think you know exactly what I was looking at." He swept me up in his arms and carried me down the hall. After he laid me on the bed he said he would be right back. A moment later he came back in the room with the whole cradle in his arms. "I would just feel better with her within eye sight." Placing Tori in the corner of the room he turned and smiled at me with a wicked smirk, "I may have to keep your mouth either full or covered so you don't wake her."

"I like the way you think baby." Despite our banter the lovemaking that night was soft and slow, he used his tongue to take my mind off my fear. And nothing could have scared me once he got started. Just as his lips circled my clit he slid two fingers inside my wet pussy. The way he moved just his fingers and not his whole hand brought me to the edge of my orgasm within seconds, he backed off and let me catch my breath; then started again! About the time I thought I couldn't take anymore he let his fingers flick my g-spot and his tongue flick my clit at the same time. I pulled the pillow over my face to muffle my scream of joy as I filled his hand and mouth with cum. I was still shaking from my release when he moved above me and slowly slid his cock inside my quivering pussy. He pushed the pillow aside and kissed me, our tongues caressing each other. Unable to breathe I turned my face away from his lips, he moved the kiss to my neck. With his cock filling my pussy, his hands holding my head and his fingers tangled in my hair; the feel of his teeth gently closing on my neck drove me into the hardest, most intense orgasm I've ever felt. I don't think that at the time I even realized I was doing it, but I turned my face away and covered my eyes so he wouldn't see the tears of emotion that flowed freely down my cheeks.

"Are you okay? Did I hurt you?" He wasn't fooled.

"I'm great, just I haven't cum like that in so long." I wrapped my arms around his neck to keep him with me. "Just silly girl emotion stuff." He kissed my lips softly and started to get up. I panicked a little. "You're staying the night right?"

His eyes softened totally, "I'll stay every night for the rest of eternity if you'll let me. But right now we need a warm wash cloth. I'll be right back."

CHAPTER 11

The next day was the BBQ. It was beautiful weather. Rick drove and we arrived about 30 mins before everyone else. I think he wanted me to have some time with Nita to relax before I met all his friends.

As usual the house was in perfect order, everything was neat and clean. Nita was in the kitchen with a glass of wine in her hand watching the oven door like she expected it to do tricks.

"What are you up to?"

She immediately took Tori out of my arms. "I was watching to make sure I didn't burn the top of the mac and cheese. You watch, I'll love on this angel. So tell me, how are things with you and Rick? He seems very happy lately."

I loved this woman, she had been my rock over the years while Rick was gone. Her shoulder absorbed more tears than I care to admit. "Everything is going great. I'm just nervous about meeting all these people today."

"All? Honey, you are confused. There's only four guys, then you, me and Sammy. How many were you expecting?"

"Really? Only 4? I was expecting more than that, not sure how many exactly, but I figured there would be wives, kids, girlfriends too."

Nita walked into the living room and placed Tori in the portable play pen she kept for when we visited. She stood staring at my sleeping child for a second. "Becca, Jon is the only one who didn't go on that last mission with the team. There were eight of them to start. Jon stayed here to handle connections and needs from this end. He added the job of watching you, and the parents of the other guys. Of the seven men that went only these four came home." She went back to the kitchen and her wine. "Rick is the first to find love. Tori will be the oldest of any of the children. You are paving new ground here kiddo. These guys didn't know how to love, they were almost scared to care about anyone or anything. Now with Burt gone, there isn't anyone left to hunt them. They can learn to relax."

I thought about that for a moment. "I just found out that Jon was part of the team. I always just thought they were friends but had no idea he was in the CIA at all. But I guess that's sorta the point. Why haven't you guys had children?"

"We were scared to. With all the craziness going on we just weren't sure if Jon would have to leave or something, then when he lost contact with the rest of the team, I don't know. I think maybe he felt like he should have been there with them. Like he felt guilty for surviving. He still holds that guilt, he doesn't feel like he's forgiven for not suffering. He seems to be softening up though. Maybe now we'll give it a shot. Who knows?"

We stood there, two women lost in our worlds, after a moment Nita smiled and we toasted 'friends and family' then drank our wine in silence. Soon the small house was filled with big strong men, the women who loved them and the slight feel of hope.

Rick stayed at her side at first and introduced her to everyone. "You know Jon and Nita Talley of course, we call him Bear. Most likely because of that mangy beard, but it could have something to do with his smell." Jon laughed and pulled Nita to his side. "Dave Stevens and Sammy Ross, I'm sure you've heard me call him Dagger,"

"Let me guess, the knives?"

"Yes, and last but not least is Jim Ray, God. Best damn sharp shooter out there. He stays at a distance and knows all the answers." Everyone laughed and the eating began!

At the first chance I had I pulled Rick aside. "I'm not trying to be nosey here but Jon is still trapped in guilt. Nita says he feels like he should have been with you guys, like he should have died with the others. Just wanted you to know."

Rick smiled at me, "I think you're going to fit in this

family perfectly. We'll talk to Jon, he has nothing to feel guilty about, he was doing exactly the job he was given, without him here to protect our loved ones we wouldn't have been able to focus."

After dinner and many many beers, the men were standing around the fire pit in the back yard talking quietly. To my surprise there was lots of hands on shoulders and even some hugs.

Nita walked up to the window "Men right." I simply smiled at her.

"Right."

Chapter 12

The morning of the rehearsal dinner Rick had the most intense feeling of dread he had ever felt. Everything with Becca was going great. The wedding plans were all set and there had been no drama with the CIA or the State Department regarding exactly how Burt Sedoris had expired or why his body had been found (along with all his files boxed neatly beside him) on the back steps of the Nashville FBI office building.

His best men Jon, Stevens and Jim all had crashed at his apartment the night before. They were all sitting in his kitchen drinking coffee and making 'dead man walking' jokes. Everything seemed squared away, but the nagging feeling would not go away.

He spent the day boxing up the rest of his stuff to move to Becca's before they left for their honeymoon the day after the wedding. He texted Becca to make sure it was all okay following her bachelorette party the night before.

He hadn't heard back. It had been about 2 hours ago. He decided to call Christy.

"Hi, how is Becca? No cold feet I hope."

"Hey Rick, I'm just parking now. I'll have her call you. Why would she leave the door open? It's hot as hell out here." He started to feel just a hint of panic. "Oh shit! Rick, get over here, looks like the office has been destroyed! I'm calling the police. She hung up before he could say anything.

"Something is wrong at Becca's, the office has been ransacked. I'm going over there." The men all tucked small pistols into their jeans, strapped on shoulder holsters and headed out the door with him.

As he drove across town Jon was calling the office. "Pull up all feed from Becca Norton's place last night and this morning. Use the computer in Rick's office, send me anything that doesn't look totally normal."

Stevens was calling the local police department, "Hey

Cody, I need a favor. I need any information you have on anything that happened in a 5-mile radius of the address 718 Blue Bird Street last night or early this morning. Send me any info you find please."

Jim was calling a contact in the local gang. "Yo man, I know it ain't our normal deal but I need to know if there was any action on Blue Bird last night. You help me out here and you and me are squared."

The scene that greeted them as they pulled up filled them with fear. Police had several of the women sitting on the steps with oxygen masks and blankets. No sign of Becca. Christy came running to him. "She's gone Rick! She and Tori and Nita. Gone!" She was trying to hold it together. He pulled her to him for a quick hug and to speak so that nobody else would hear. "I need you to look in her linen closet that faces the living room, there is a metal box sitting on the floor of that closet, I need you to unplug the wires from the back and bring me the metal box." When she just looked at him he leaned back to make eye contact. "Christy, you can fall apart when I bring them home but for now I need that box."

She nodded and headed back into the building. The men had scattered to gather what info they could. Jon was the first to come back to him, "There was one man, tall, thin, dirty black hair, no accent. According to the women he kicked the door in, grabbed Tori and started to run, Becca hit him with something, he held the gun on her and made Nita tie up the other women, then took Becca, Nita and the baby with him."

Christy ran back to Rick with a large bag on her shoulder. "Ok, here's the box. Find her and kill whoever took her."

Rick took the bag. "I'll get her, you hold things down here and take care of the others. I'll call you as soon as I have her."

Jim walked up still on the phone, "ok, word on the

street is he is holed up at an abandoned apartment building in south Nashville. I have an address let's go."

Stevens piped up, "PD is on the way to the address you gave me."

"What's the box Ghost?"

"Just an old dehumidifier, I needed her to have a purpose. She's no good to the other women if she's melting down."

The team climbed back in the jeep and took off downtown. Once they pulled up outside the building Rick started barking orders. "God, I need eyes on the side of that building, use the fire escapes, get me a solid floor number. Bear, grab your kit and follow God. Dagger, load up you have the front I'll take the back." Rick looked down for a second. "These women are part of us men, that's Bear's wife and my fiancé and daughter up there, we don't know what we're walking into but we are bringing everyone home today."

The men placed their hands-on Rick's shoulder for a split second before running to their assigned location. Within seconds God was on the radio, "Ghost, head to second base, Bear's bringing band aids." Rick and Jon immediately headed to the second floor keeping an eye out for blood. There were only 6 apartments but they didn't have to worry about searching them, only one had a trail of blood leading from the landing and under the door.

Rage slammed into Rick and he rushed the door. Before he made contact with the wood he heard a woman's voice yell, "On your face ass hole!" a shot rang out and Rick's stomach dropped out. Going through the door he stopped dead in his tracks. Becca was standing with her back toward the door and a gun in her hand, she was looking at something on the floor in front of her. Nita was sitting in the corner behind her with Tori in her arms screaming at the top of her little lungs.

He slowly crept forward til he saw the man laying on

the floor. "Becky, give me the gun baby." Rick reached for the gun, she handed it to him without a fight. Jon moved toward the man and seeing he didn't have a weapon knelt beside him to assess the damage. Rick pulled Becca to him and wrapped his arms around her. She looked up into his eyes and the fear he saw behind her eyes melted as she leaned into his embrace.

"Ghost, he's alive. Damn girl you put a nasty hole in his shoulder, but he'll talk."

Becca's head lifted and she ripped herself out of Rick's arms, he reached for her but she reached the man before Rick could get a good grip on her.

"Who the hell are you?" Becca kicked him in the shoulder, she bent down and slapped him. "Wake up asshole, I want answers!"

Rick pulled her away from him. "I got this baby. Get Tori and Nita and go outside, Dagger is there. Let me take care of this. Go call Christy, she's worried sick."

"Rick, I want his fucking head on a platter along with whoever put him up to this. I don't care if you have to kill everyone he knows." She took her crying child and the two women left the apartment.

"Alright dumbass, this is your only chance to tell me what the hell you are doing kidnapping innocent women and children. Who sent you?"

"Innocent?? That bitch stole my daughter! She waited til I was in jail, then she and that stupid cow I knocked up stole my child from me."

Rick took a step back. This idiot wasn't tied to his life at all. He had not brought this danger to his family. Suddenly Rick started laughing, it was only a few seconds before Jon joined him. "Boy you just ain't got a clue how much shit you just stepped in." Pulling the guy up by his injured shoulder Rick pushed him out the door of the apartment and into the waiting company of the police department. "I believe this idiot belongs to you, not me.

But if you could do me a personal favor and put him in maximum security this time, and maybe under the prison."

Rick and Jon walked over to where the women stood with the rest of the men. His team, his fiancé, his daughter, his family.

Wedding Day

September 23rd, I look at the gathering of our friends and families. In a few minutes I'd walk down the flowered path to marry the man of my dreams, finally! Gazing at Rick waiting for me, I breathe a sigh of relief, finally everything will be alright. Not perfect I know that, but we'll be together. The music starts and he looks up and meets my eyes. I melt.

"I now pronounce you husband and wife. You may kiss the bride."

Finally, as Mr. and Mrs. Rick Dorsey. We kissed deeply and with all the promise of newlyweds. I smile at my new husband. He looks at me then looks at Tori in my mom's arms. "How do you like being daddy so far?"

"It's great. I can't wait til we have more."

"Would you be okay with having more kids sooner rather than later.?

"As soon as possible is great with me."

"Good, cause you only have to wait seven months."

"Are you sure?" He took Tori and held her sleeping form in the crook of his elbow.

"Yes, I went to the doctor a few days ago." He hugged Tori and I close.

"You two have made me the happiest man in the world."

Hint of something cumming soon....

Long Hard Ride to Heaven

Theana Stephos

Theana looked out her kitchen window, the wide open field behind the little house was her newest 'happy place'. Off to the left she could see the fence of the main barn yard. Karma, her palamino stallion was eating with the rest of the horses. She couldn't help but wish this could be her reality forever. Sighing, Theana put her coffee cup in the sink and headed for work.

St. Francis Medical Center, Theana's latest home away from home. Being a nurse is the only thing that keeps her going; and she loves this hospital. Working in the ER gives her the excitement she needs and provides very little time to get to know the people she works with. Makes it easier when it's time to leave.

"Hey Thea, thought you were going on vacation?" Kyra is the closest Theana has come to a best friend in 5 years, and the only one on the planet who knew the whole story.

"I am. Tonight is my last shift for 5 whole days!"

"Are you going anywhere?" Kyra gave her a look that asked the question on a much deeper level.

"No, just staying at the ranch. The owner and his wife are taking off for a week to check out a horse auction so I'll have the whole recreation area to myself. I'm going to ride Karma, lay by the pool and read a trashy romance."

"Sounds fabulous! I may join you by the pool one day."

"Come on out. I won't be going anywhere." Shift changed and the influx of patients got in the way of any more conversation. With any luck there would be very little drama and she would be home by 11:15 and out on Karma under the stars by midnight!

Micah Flynt

"Colorado? Are you freaking nuts? What the hell is way out there in the middle of nowhere that you need?"

Dave and Micah had been through hell and back together, and now that it was time to retire neither relished the idea of being away from the other. "My parent's ranch is in Colorado Springs, my land is attached to theirs, the hospital I want to work in is there. Come on man, wide open space, fresh air, all that crap." At his friend's look he decided to try one more time. "Look, where else are you gonna go? You been watching my back for almost 20 years, your parents are gone, nobody claims your butt except me. Half my land is yours, hell I'll even help you build a damn house."

Dave punched him in the shoulder. "I'll think about it ok? I'm going to roam around and see my own country for a change. But I plan to take you up on the house building thing. How far out is this land of yours anyway?"

"Far enough, plenty of room for a range and I can see anyone coming for miles."

"Ok, I'll come out there in a few months. There are a few places I've never been that I'd like to see before I give up my traveling ways."

ABOUT THE AUTHOR

Lorrain Everett is a divorced mother of 2 amazing teenagers, she works full time as a nurse and spends as much time writing as she can. She bounces ideas off her best friend, her ex-husband and her inner romantic. She can be found on the web at lorraineverett.com or on facebook at Lorrain Everett – author